ROD SERLING's THE TWILIGHT ZONE

WALKING DISTANCE

Adaptation from Rod Serling's original script by

MARK KNEECE

Illustrated by

DOVE McHARGUE

WALKER & COMPANY
NEW YORK

INTRODUCTION

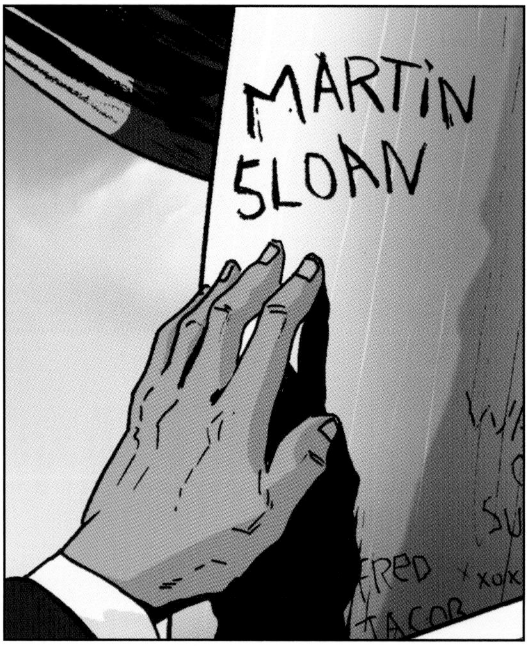
MARTIN
SLOAN
FRED

There is a fifth dimension beyond that which is known to man. It is a dimension as vast as space and timeless as infinity. It is the middle ground between light and shadow, between science and superstition, and it lies between the pit of man's fears and the summit of his knowledge. This is the dimension of imagination. It is an area which we call the Twilight Zone.

America, between the 1950s and early 1960s, was itself in a sort of "twilight zone." Following the victories of World War II and the attending economic boom—but before the Civil Rights marches; the assassinations of John F. Kennedy, Martin Luther King, Jr., and Robert F. Kennedy; and the Vietnam War—we were wrapped in a gleaming package of shining chrome, white picket fences, and Hollywood glamour. But beneath this shimmering facade lay a turbulent core of racial inequality, sexual inequality, and the Cold War threat of nuclear attacks from the Soviet Union. We'd never been more affluent—or more frightened.

Enter Rodman Edward Serling of Binghamton, New York. Serling began writing in his teens for his high school newspaper; as a student at Antioch College, he was already selling scripts to radio programs. While serving as a paratrooper in the U.S. Army Eleventh Airborne (for which he earned a Purple Heart), he wrote for the Armed Services Radio. He went on to write for film and television, first in feature presentations for *Hallmark Hall of Fame* and *Playhouse 90,* including the lauded "Requiem for a Heavyweight," perhaps drawing inspiration from his own experiences as a Golden Gloves boxer. More than two hundred of his teleplays were produced. In all, his work would win not only the adoration of listeners and viewers but a host of prestigious awards, including a record-breaking six Emmy awards—two of them for his greatest achievement, *The Twilight Zone*.

The worlds and characters presented over the course of five seasons, beginning in October 1959, were like nothing audiences had seen before. Television, the new "must have" appliance for America's increasingly prosperous households, offered comedies such as *I Love Lucy* and *The Honeymooners*, news programs including Edward R. Murrow's *See It Now*, as well as Westerns, game shows, and soap operas. With a typewriter as his spade, Serling dug beneath the surface of the expected and planted the seeds of a more imaginative and thoughtful genre, writing more than half of the show's 156 episodes while producing and hosting all of them. He bravely took on themes of oppression, prejudice, and paranoia, all the while giving people what they needed at the end of the day: entertainment.

While he had his run-ins with censorship, Serling's clever use of other worlds and veiled scenarios generally protected him. As he explained, what he couldn't have a Republican or a Democrat espouse on the show, he could have an alien profess without offending the sponsors. This approach also allowed viewers to take away whatever message best suited them; the more reflective could consider the psychological and political implications, while others might be satisfied with simply enjoying the thrill of the surface story. So much more than mere science fiction or fantasy, Serling's scripts are parables that explore the multifaceted natures of hope, fear, humanity, loneliness, and self-delusion.

Half a century later, *The Twilight Zone* remains a part of our culture, routinely referenced in print and on television, having become a shorthand expression that succinctly describes the bizarre and unexpected. The original episodes are still aired on the SciFi Channel, both in late-night slots and as day-long marathons. The show was literally a Who's Who of Hollywood, helping to foster the careers of fledgling actors including Robert Redford, Ron Howard, Dennis Hopper, Charles Bronson, and William Shatner. It has also inspired countless authors and filmmakers, who have gone on to break through boundaries of their own.

In the fifty years since *The Twilight Zone* first aired, we've faced new enemies and have altered our definitions of happiness, but our core hopes and fears remain the same, as does our desire to be entertained. The stories are as compelling, and as telling, as ever. And now, in their newest incarnation, Serling's scripts serve as the basis for this graphic novel series, which honors the original text and even echoes the storyboarding of television, but offers a fresh interpretation, as seen through the eyes of a new generation of artists.

—Anna Marlis Burgard
Director of Industry Partnerships, Savannah College of Art and Design

You're traveling through

another dimension,

a dimension not only of sight and sound

but of mind;

a journey into a wondrous land

whose boundaries

are that of imagination.

That's the signpost up ahead—

your next stop,

the Twilight Zone!

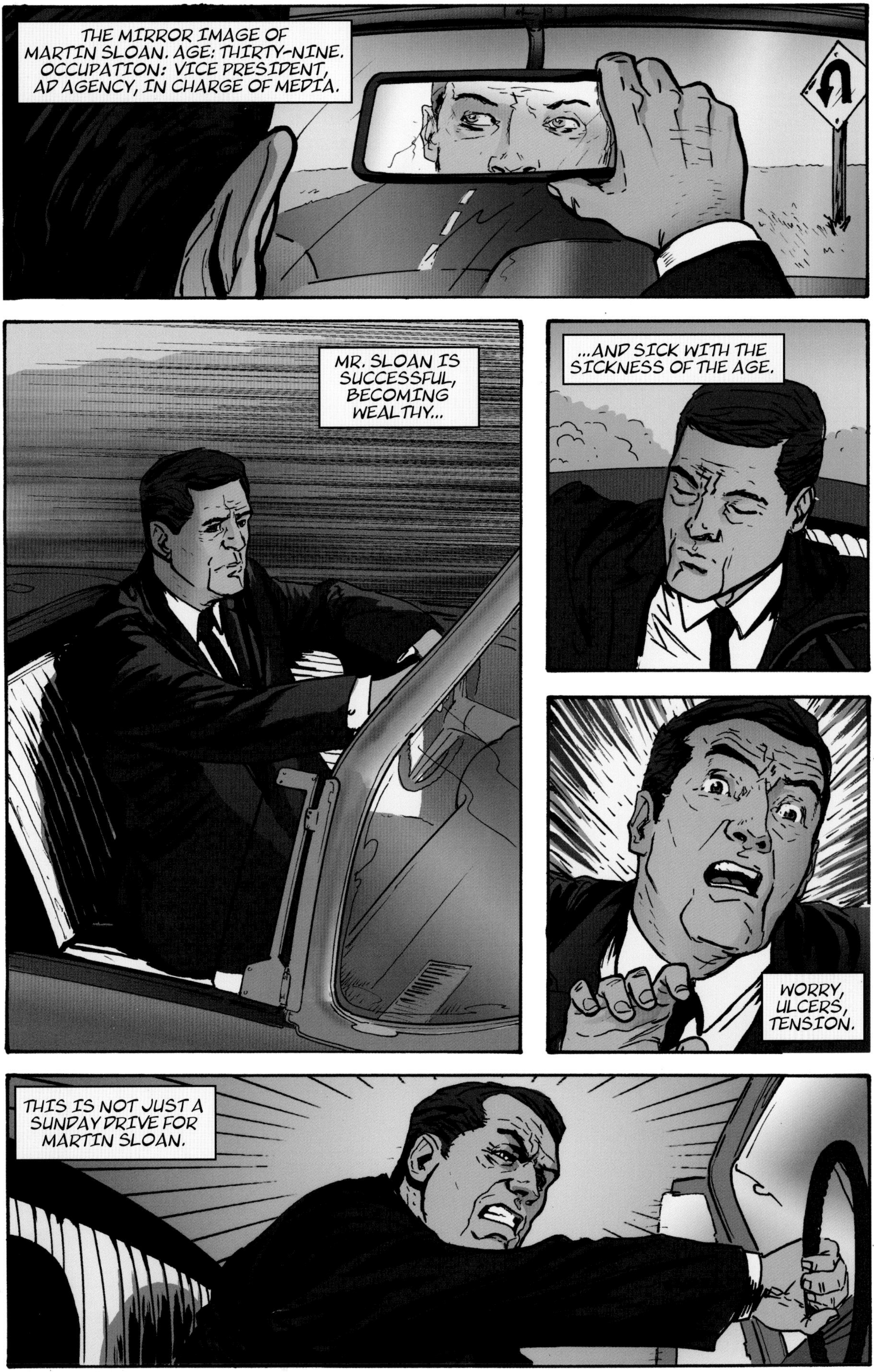
THE MIRROR IMAGE OF MARTIN SLOAN. AGE: THIRTY-NINE. OCCUPATION: VICE PRESIDENT, AD AGENCY, IN CHARGE OF MEDIA.
MR. SLOAN IS SUCCESSFUL, BECOMING WEALTHY...
...AND SICK WITH THE SICKNESS OF THE AGE.
WORRY, ULCERS, TENSION.
THIS IS NOT JUST A SUNDAY DRIVE FOR MARTIN SLOAN.

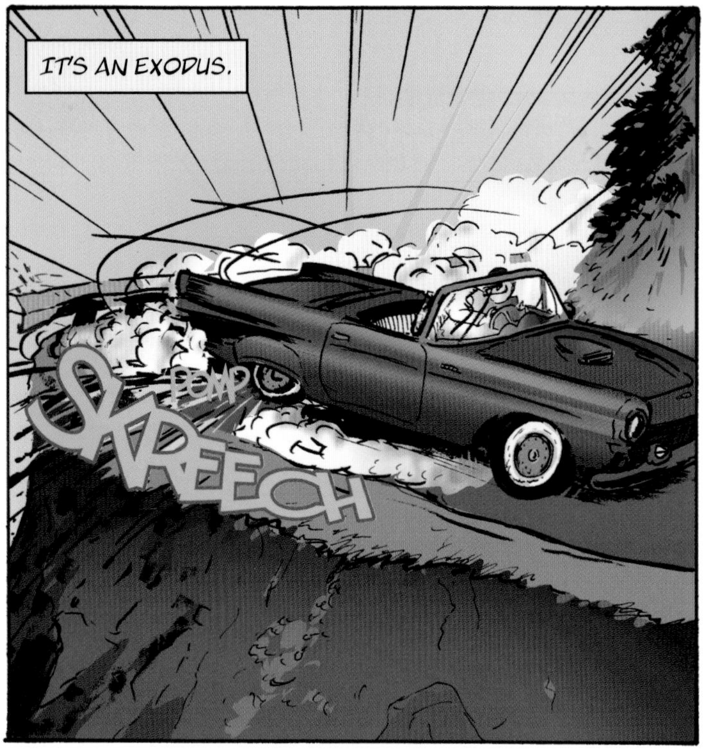
IT'S AN EXODUS.
SKREECH

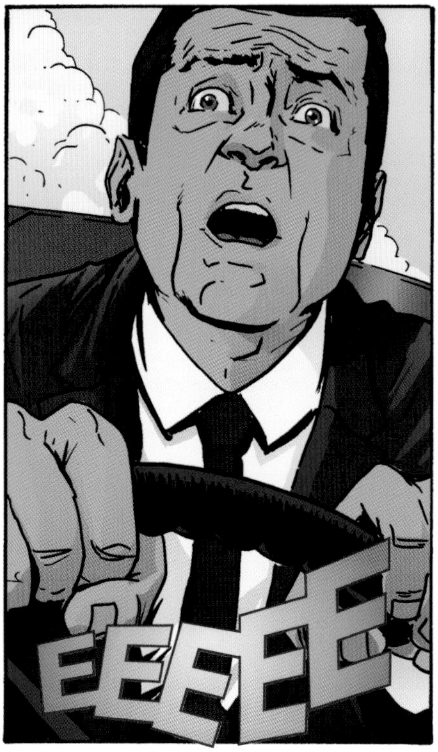
EEEEE

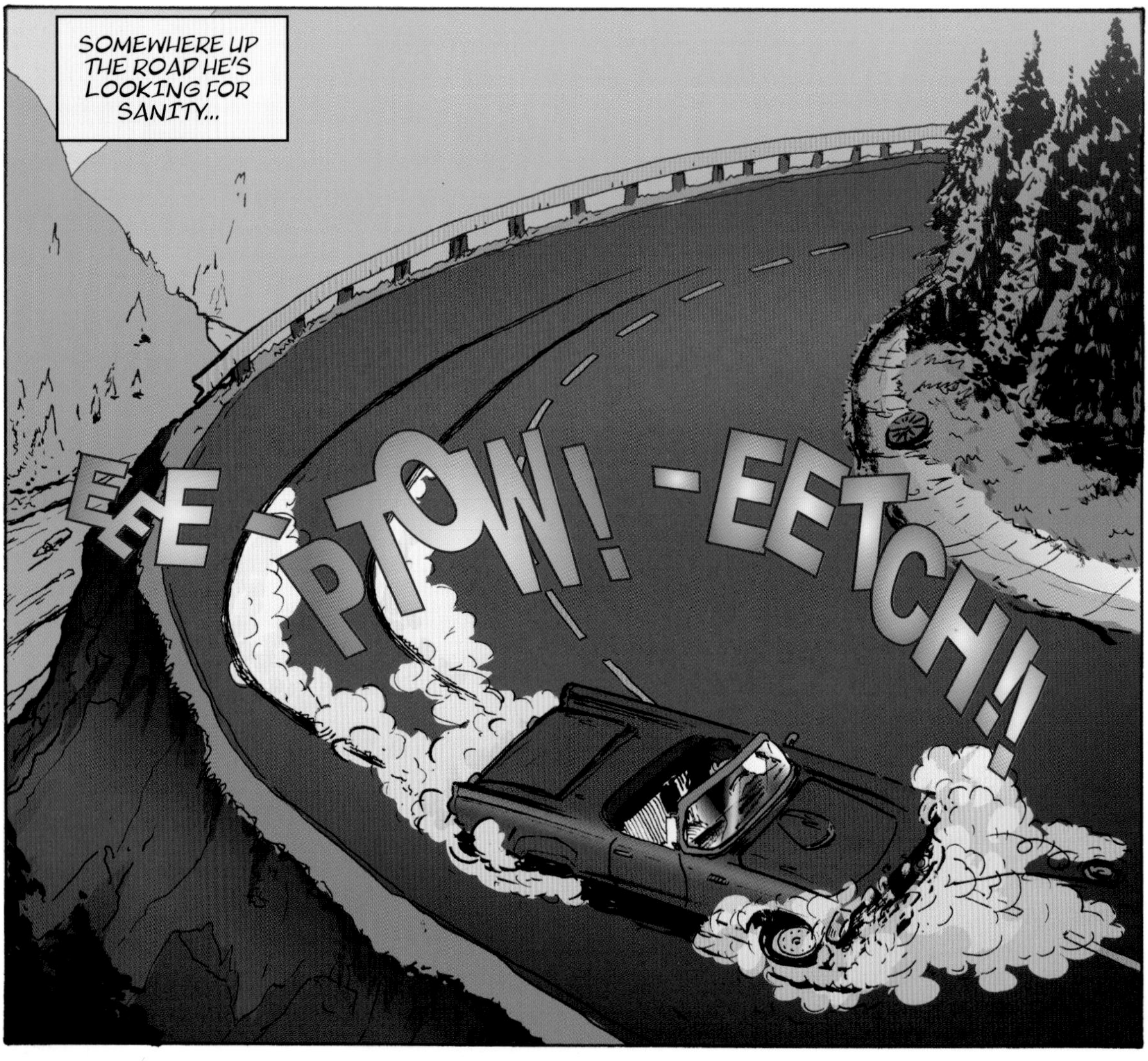
SOMEWHERE UP THE ROAD HE'S LOOKING FOR SANITY...
EEE-PTOW! -EETCH!!

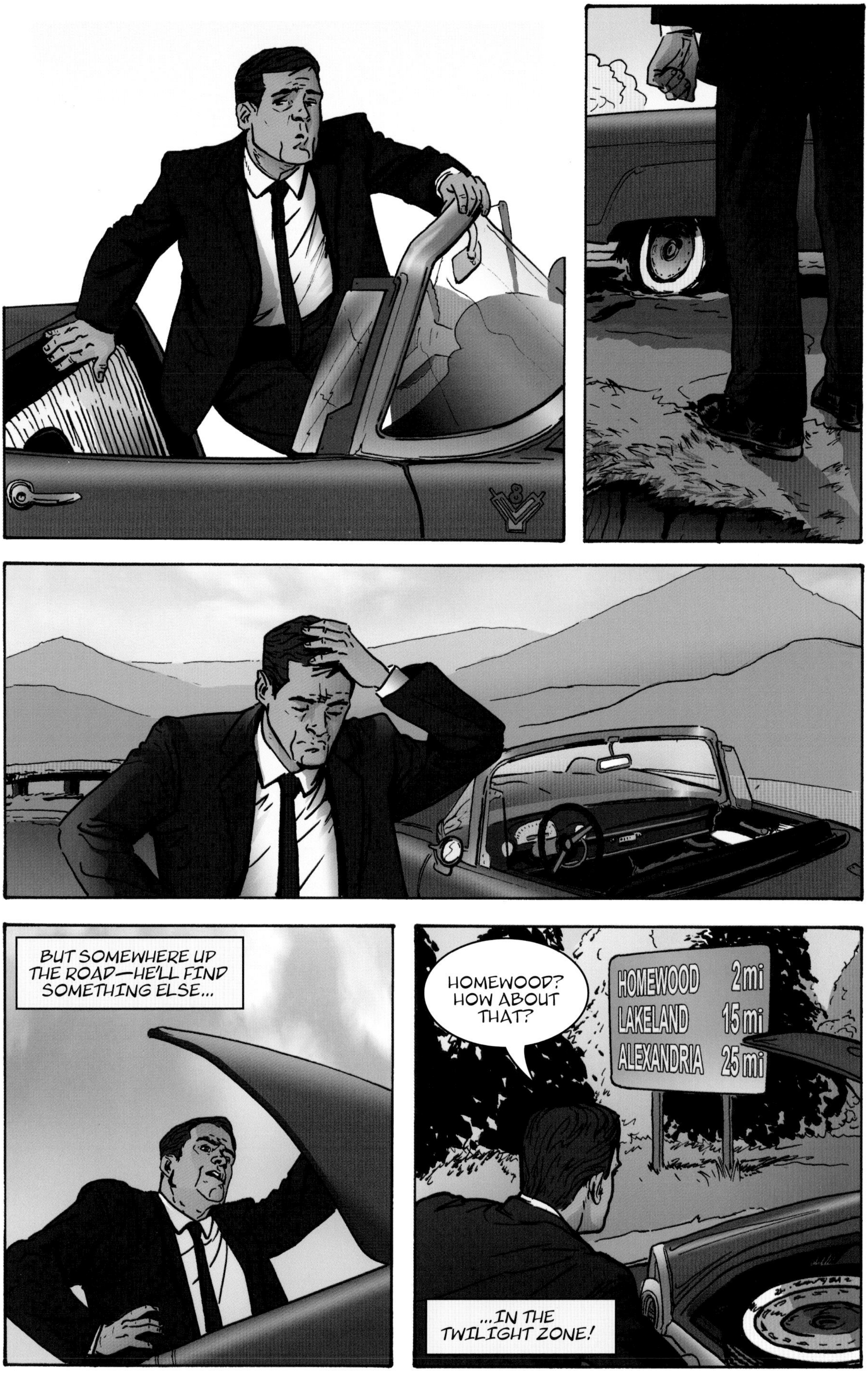
BUT SOMEWHERE UP THE ROAD—HE'LL FIND SOMETHING ELSE...
HOMEWOOD? HOW ABOUT THAT?
HOMEWOOD 2 mi
LAKELAND 15 mi
ALEXANDRIA 25 mi
...IN THE TWILIGHT ZONE!

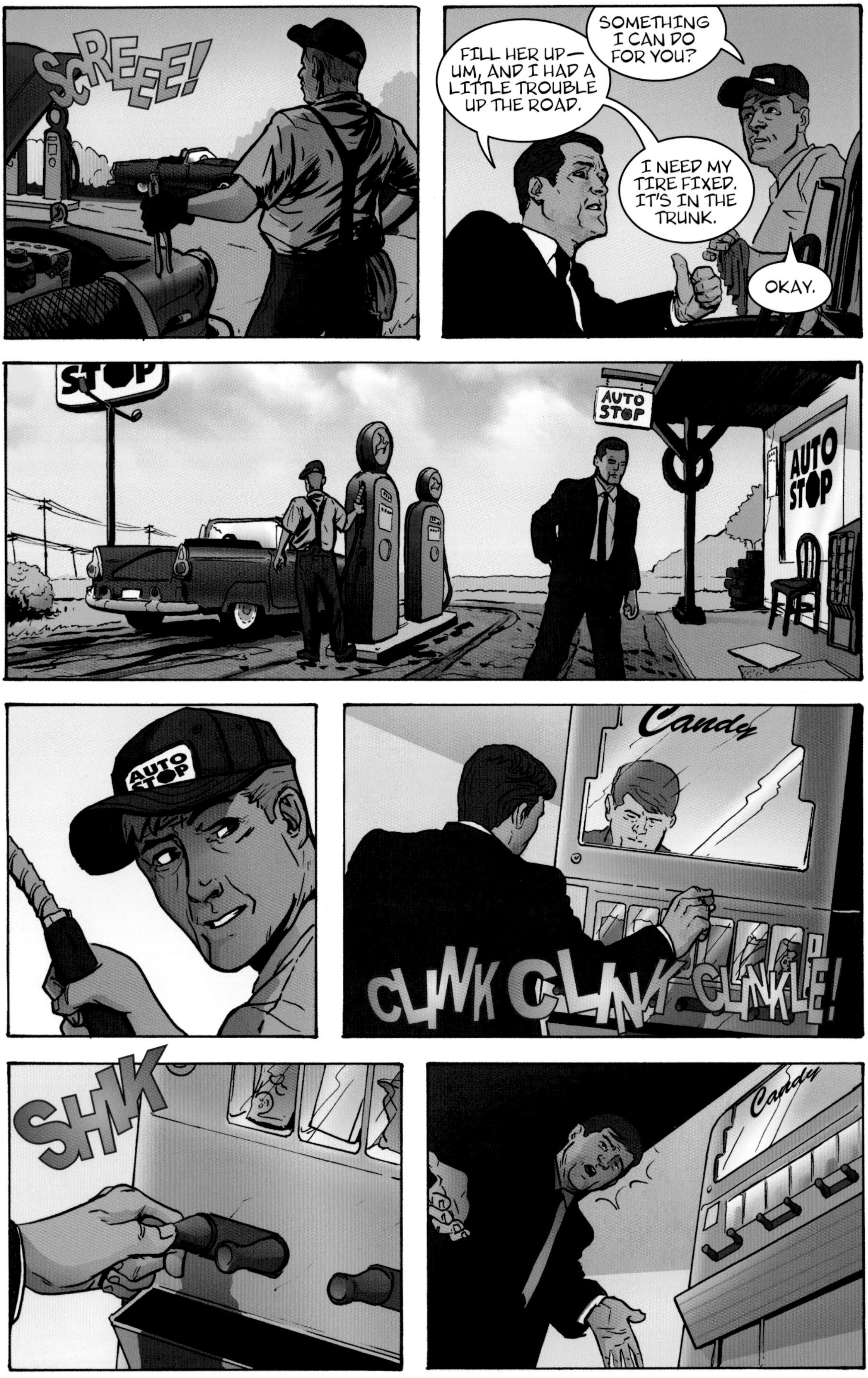
SCREEEE!
SOMETHING I CAN DO FOR YOU?
FILL HER UP— UM, AND I HAD A LITTLE TROUBLE UP THE ROAD.
I NEED MY TIRE FIXED. IT'S IN THE TRUNK.
OKAY.
STOP
AUTO STOP
AUTO STOP
AUTO STOP
Candy
CLINK CLINK CLINKLE!
SHIK
Candy

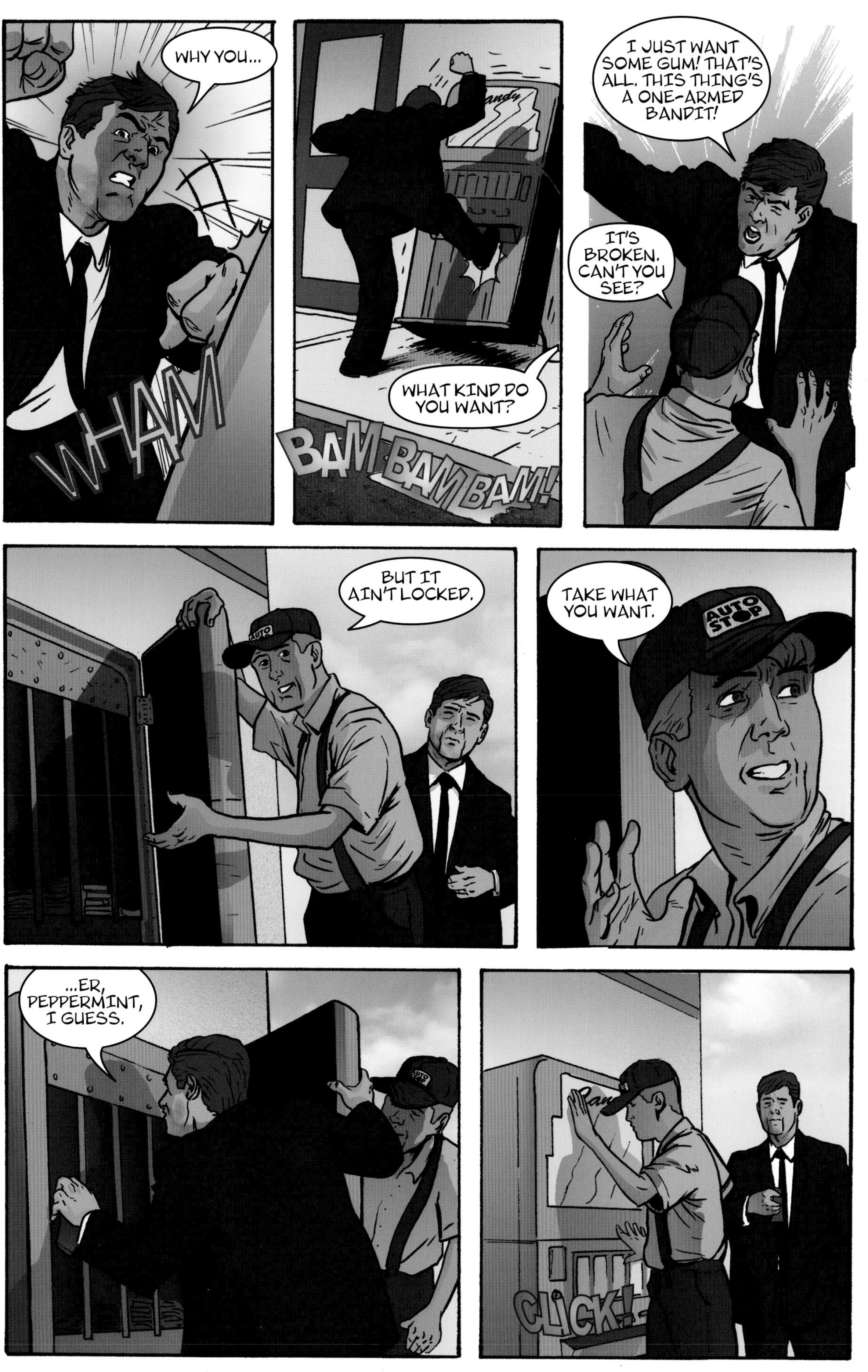
WHY YOU...
WHAM
WHAT KIND DO YOU WANT?
BAM BAM BAM!
I JUST WANT SOME GUM! THAT'S ALL. THIS THING'S A ONE-ARMED BANDIT!
IT'S BROKEN. CAN'T YOU SEE?
BUT IT AIN'T LOCKED.
TAKE WHAT YOU WANT.
AUTO STOP
...ER, PEPPERMINT, I GUESS.
CLICK!

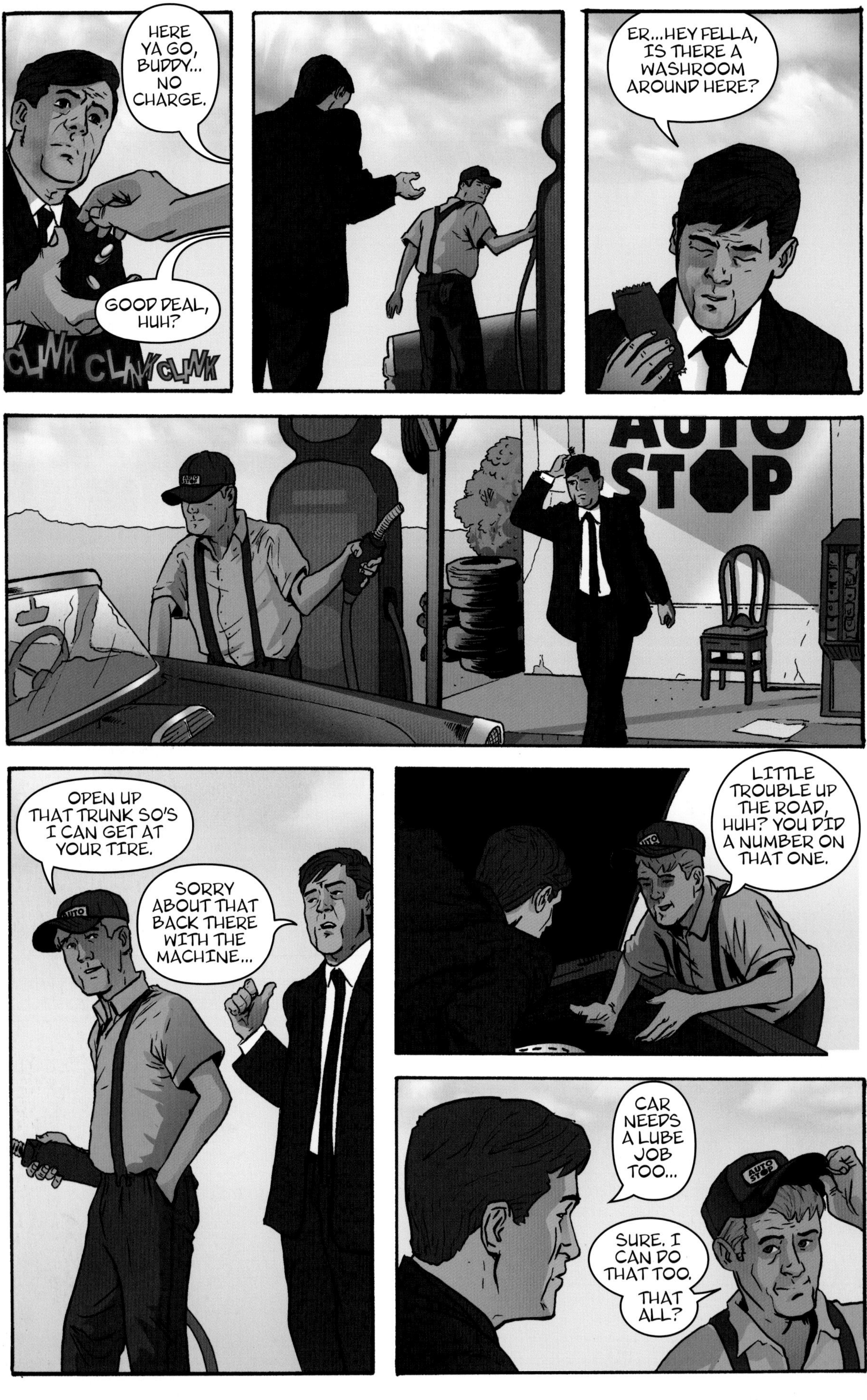
HERE YA GO, BUDDY... NO CHARGE.
GOOD DEAL, HUH?
CLINK CLINK CLINK
ER...HEY FELLA, IS THERE A WASHROOM AROUND HERE?
AUTO STOP
OPEN UP THAT TRUNK SO'S I CAN GET AT YOUR TIRE.
SORRY ABOUT THAT BACK THERE WITH THE MACHINE...
LITTLE TROUBLE UP THE ROAD, HUH? YOU DID A NUMBER ON THAT ONE.
CAR NEEDS A LUBE JOB TOO...
SURE. I CAN DO THAT TOO.
THAT ALL?

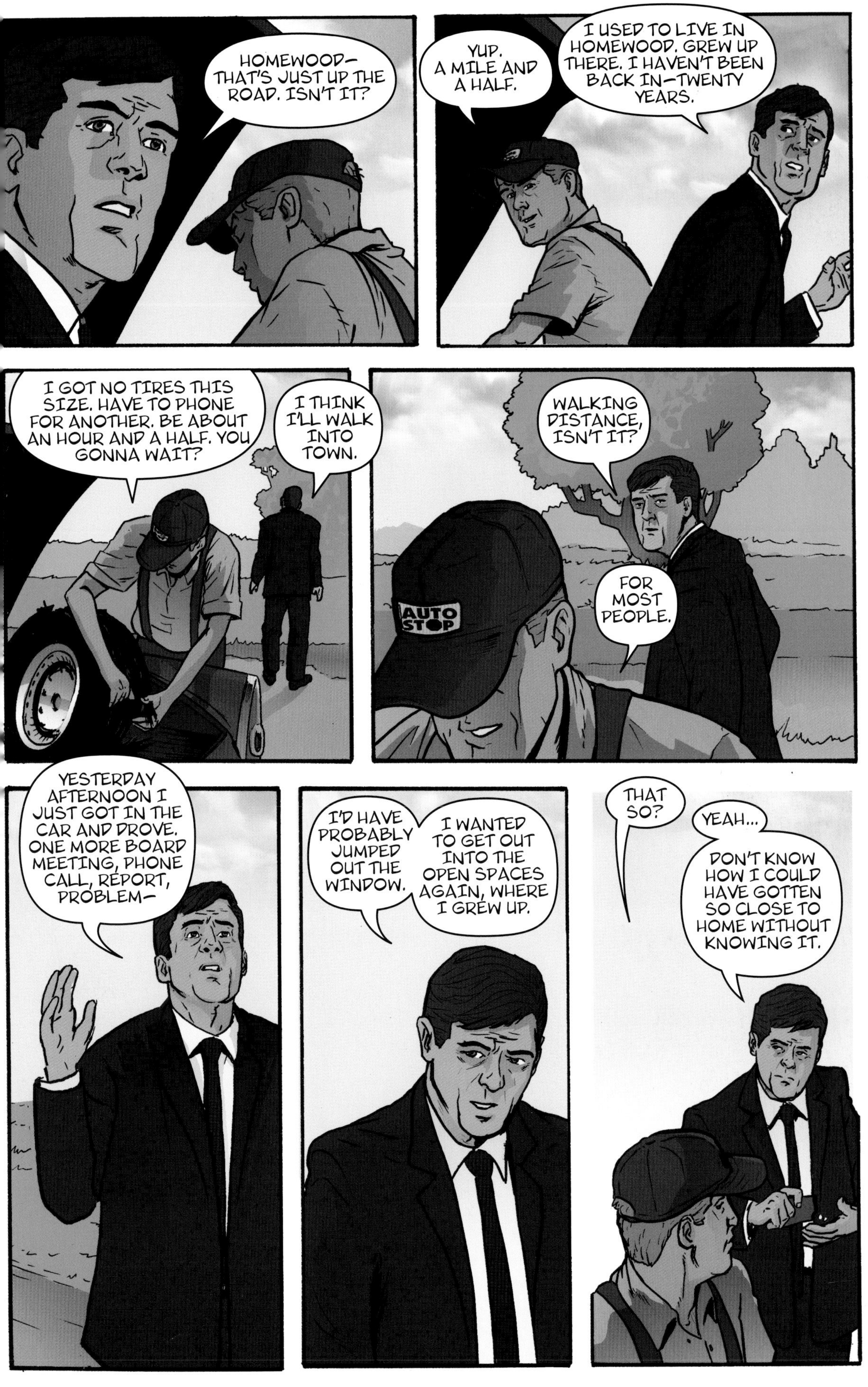
HOMEWOOD—THAT'S JUST UP THE ROAD. ISN'T IT?
YUP. A MILE AND A HALF.
I USED TO LIVE IN HOMEWOOD. GREW UP THERE. I HAVEN'T BEEN BACK IN—TWENTY YEARS.
I GOT NO TIRES THIS SIZE. HAVE TO PHONE FOR ANOTHER. BE ABOUT AN HOUR AND A HALF. YOU GONNA WAIT?
I THINK I'LL WALK INTO TOWN.
WALKING DISTANCE, ISN'T IT?
AUTO STOP
FOR MOST PEOPLE.
YESTERDAY AFTERNOON I JUST GOT IN THE CAR AND DROVE. ONE MORE BOARD MEETING, PHONE CALL, REPORT, PROBLEM—
I'D HAVE PROBABLY JUMPED OUT THE WINDOW.
I WANTED TO GET OUT INTO THE OPEN SPACES AGAIN, WHERE I GREW UP.
THAT SO?
YEAH...
DON'T KNOW HOW I COULD HAVE GOTTEN SO CLOSE TO HOME WITHOUT KNOWING IT.

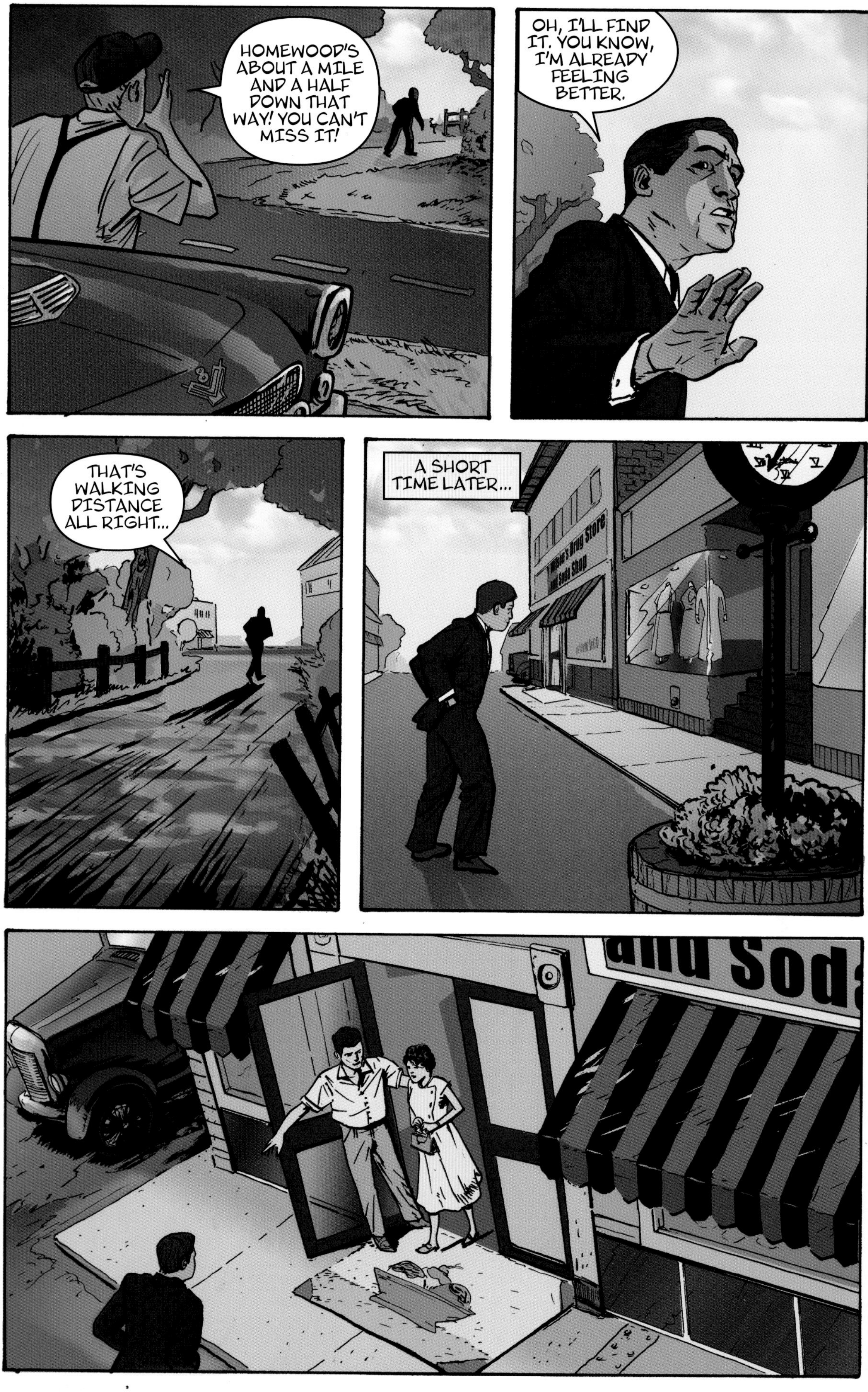
HOMEWOOD'S ABOUT A MILE AND A HALF DOWN THAT WAY! YOU CAN'T MISS IT!
OH, I'LL FIND IT. YOU KNOW, I'M ALREADY FEELING BETTER.
THAT'S WALKING DISTANCE ALL RIGHT...
A SHORT TIME LATER...
and Soda

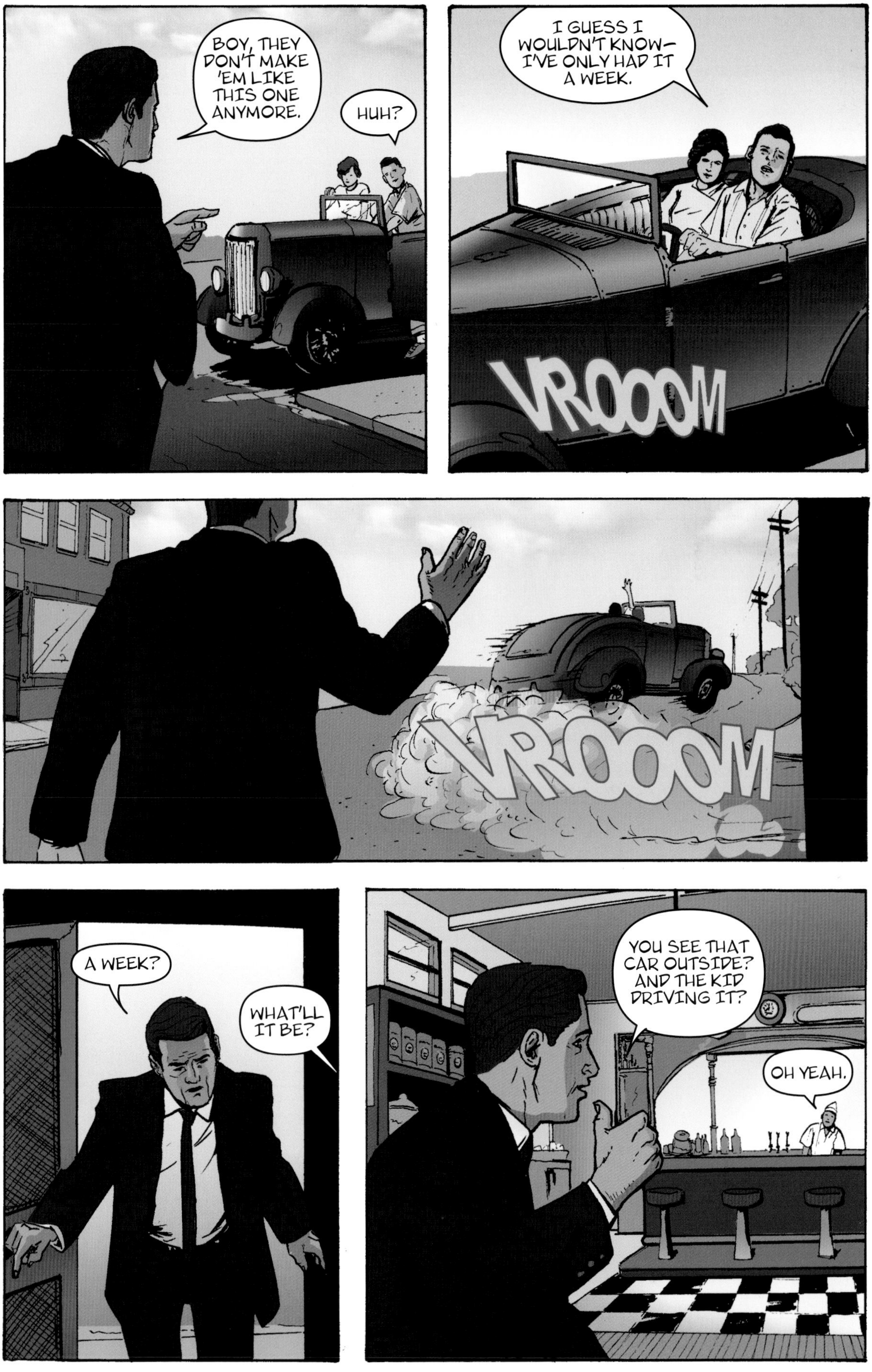
BOY, THEY DON'T MAKE 'EM LIKE THIS ONE ANYMORE.
HUH?
I GUESS I WOULDN'T KNOW— I'VE ONLY HAD IT A WEEK.
VROOOM
VROOOM
A WEEK?
WHAT'LL IT BE?
YOU SEE THAT CAR OUTSIDE? AND THE KID DRIVING IT?
OH YEAH.

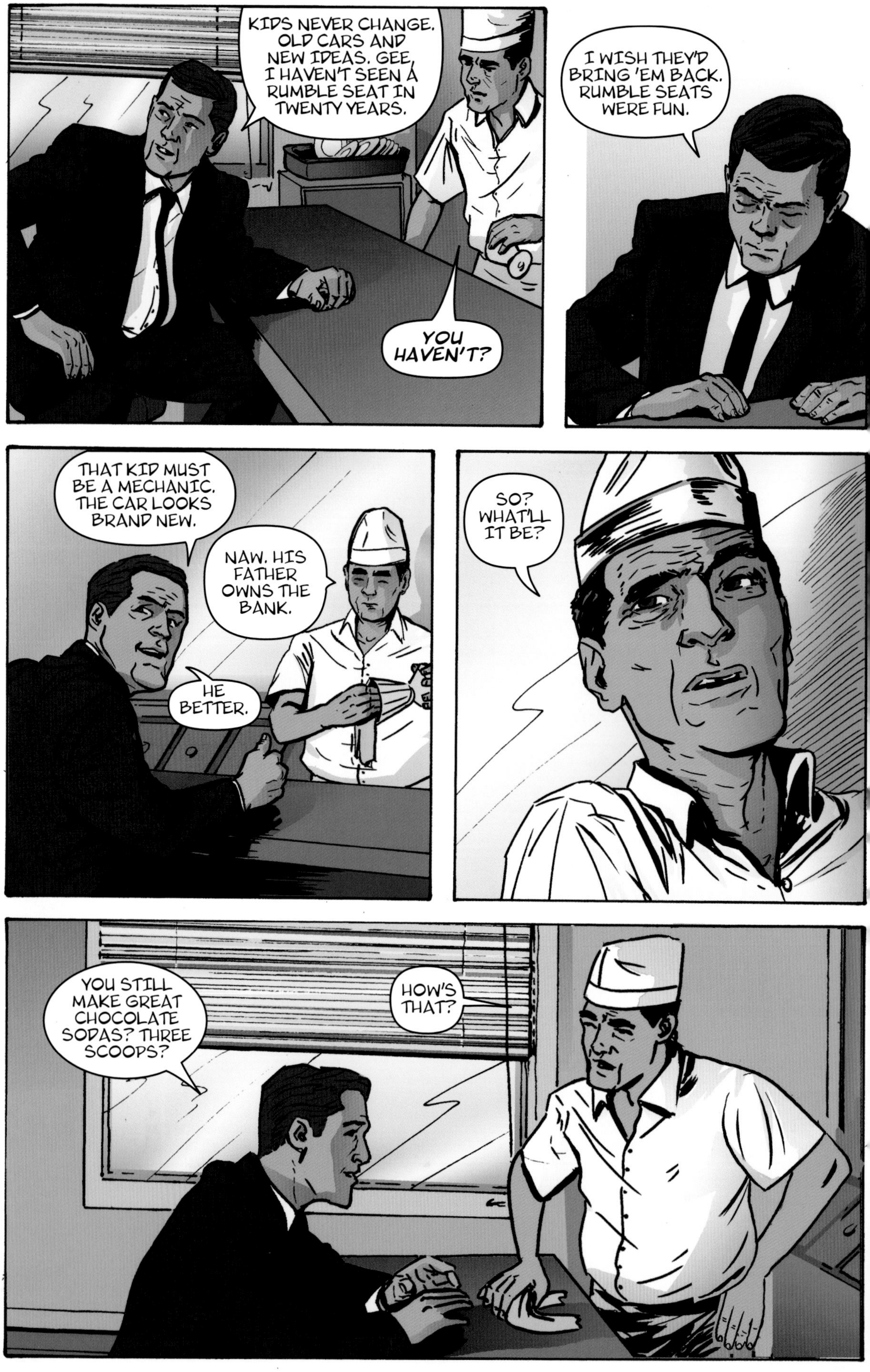
KIDS NEVER CHANGE. OLD CARS AND NEW IDEAS. GEE, I HAVEN'T SEEN A RUMBLE SEAT IN TWENTY YEARS.
YOU HAVEN'T?
I WISH THEY'D BRING 'EM BACK. RUMBLE SEATS WERE FUN.
THAT KID MUST BE A MECHANIC. THE CAR LOOKS BRAND NEW.
NAW. HIS FATHER OWNS THE BANK.
HE BETTER.
SO? WHAT'LL IT BE?
YOU STILL MAKE GREAT CHOCOLATE SODAS? THREE SCOOPS?
HOW'S THAT?

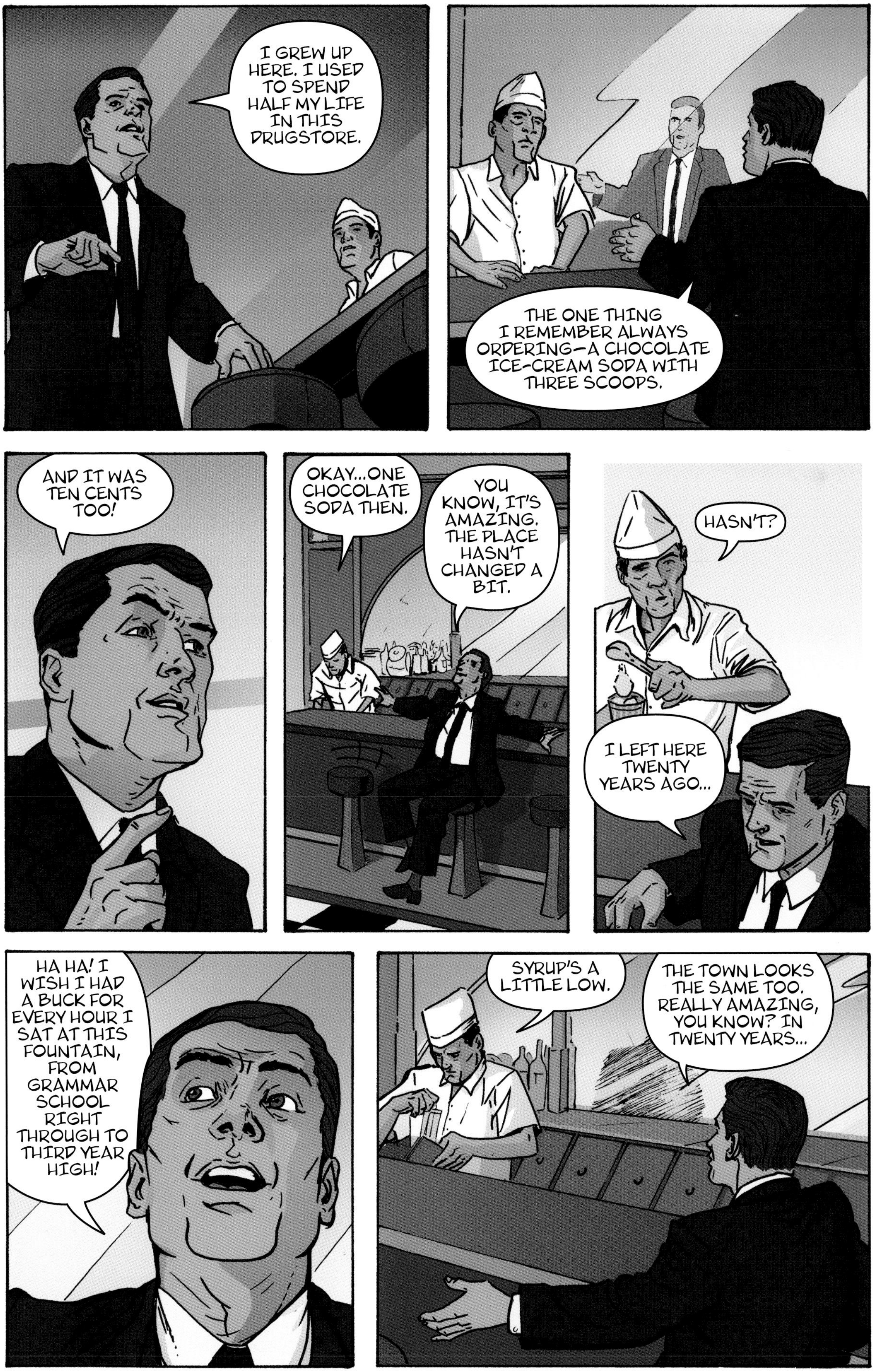
I GREW UP HERE. I USED TO SPEND HALF MY LIFE IN THIS DRUGSTORE.
THE ONE THING I REMEMBER ALWAYS ORDERING—A CHOCOLATE ICE-CREAM SODA WITH THREE SCOOPS.
AND IT WAS TEN CENTS TOO!
OKAY...ONE CHOCOLATE SODA THEN.
YOU KNOW, IT'S AMAZING. THE PLACE HASN'T CHANGED A BIT.
HASN'T?
I LEFT HERE TWENTY YEARS AGO...
HA HA! I WISH I HAD A BUCK FOR EVERY HOUR I SAT AT THIS FOUNTAIN, FROM GRAMMAR SCHOOL RIGHT THROUGH TO THIRD YEAR HIGH!
SYRUP'S A LITTLE LOW.
THE TOWN LOOKS THE SAME TOO. REALLY AMAZING, YOU KNOW? IN TWENTY YEARS...

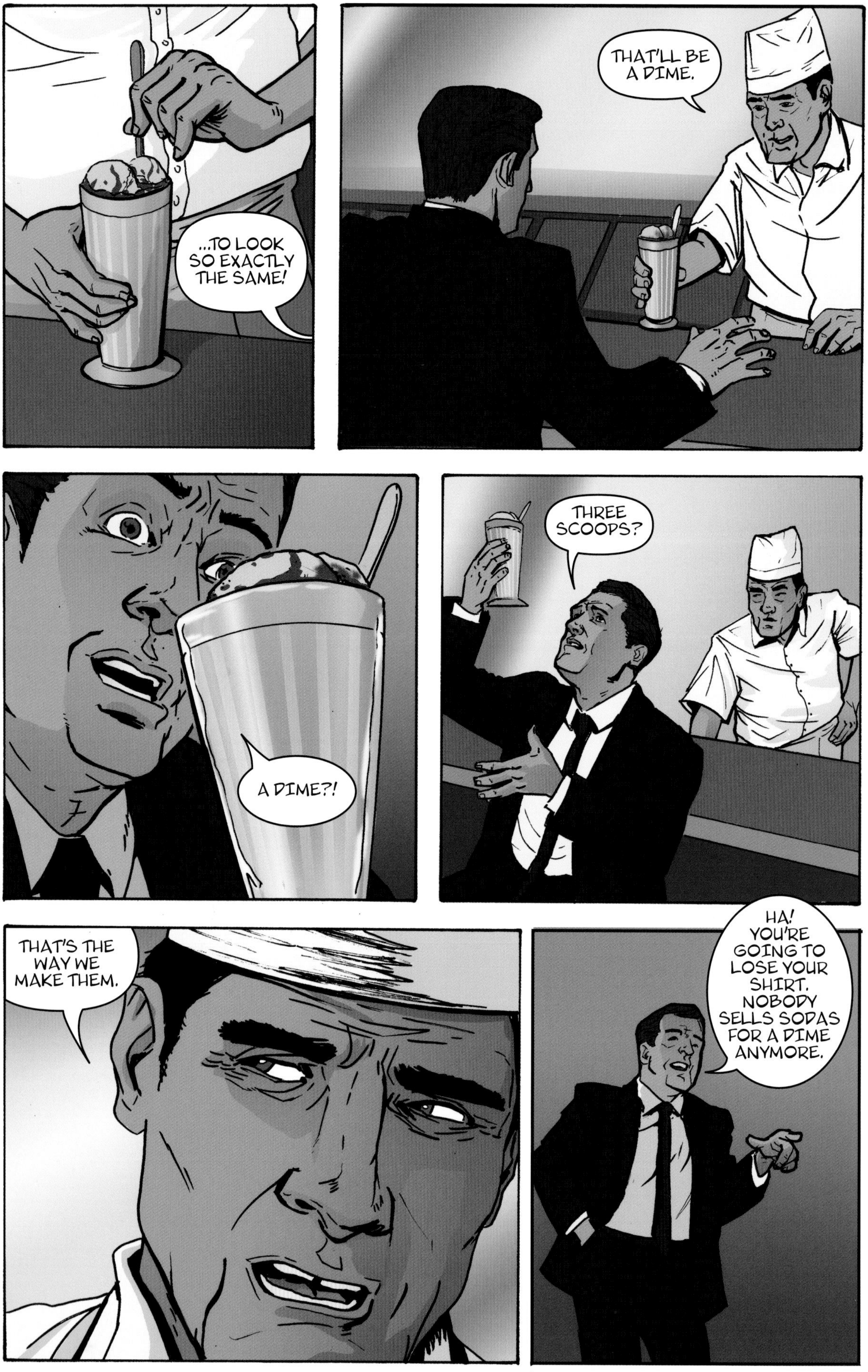
...TO LOOK SO EXACTLY THE SAME!
THAT'LL BE A DIME.
A DIME?!
THREE SCOOPS?
THAT'S THE WAY WE MAKE THEM.
HA! YOU'RE GOING TO LOSE YOUR SHIRT. NOBODY SELLS SODAS FOR A DIME ANYMORE.

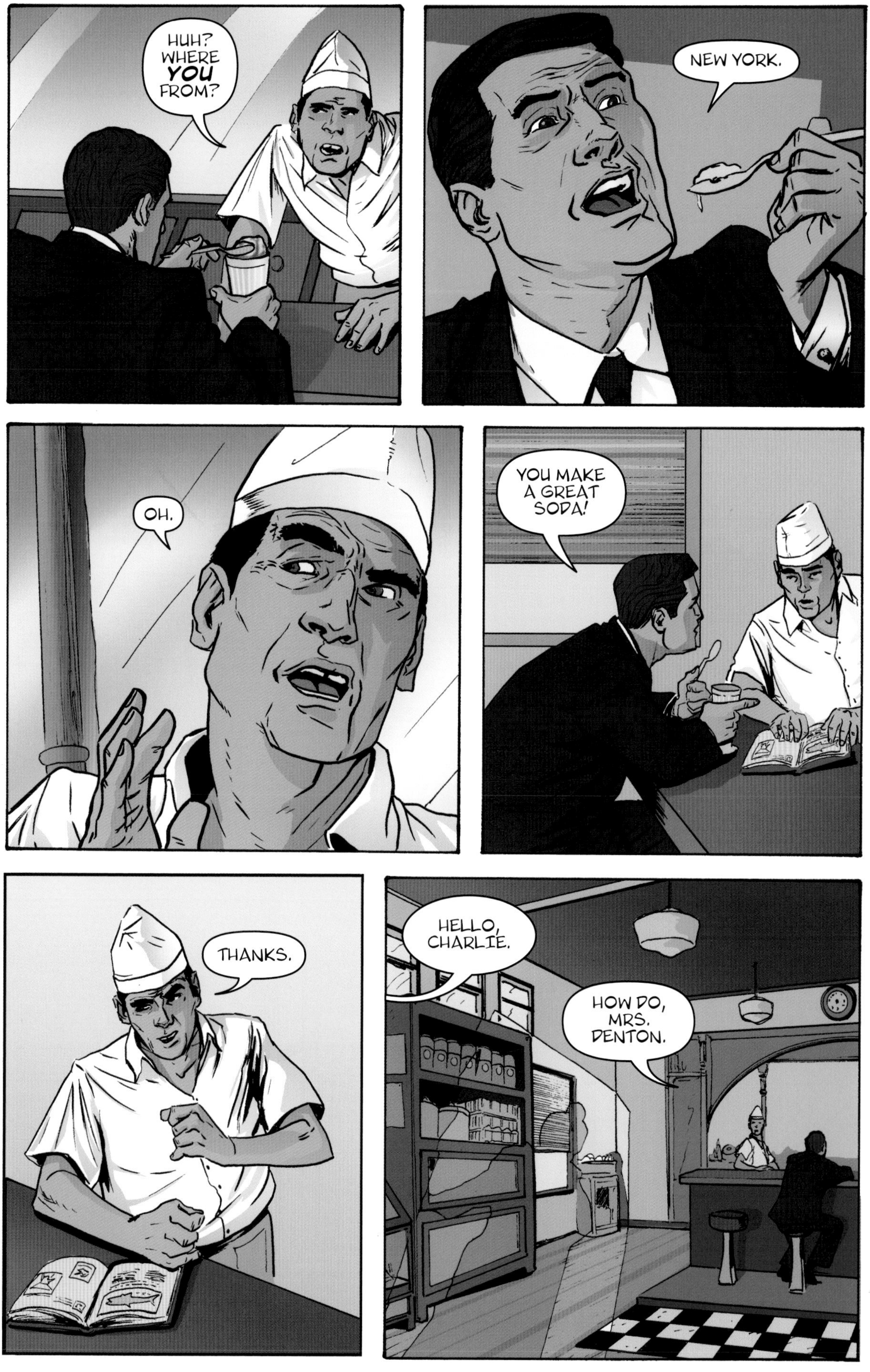
HUH? WHERE **YOU** FROM?
NEW YORK.
OH.
YOU MAKE A GREAT SODA!
THANKS.
HELLO, CHARLIE.
HOW DO, MRS. DENTON.

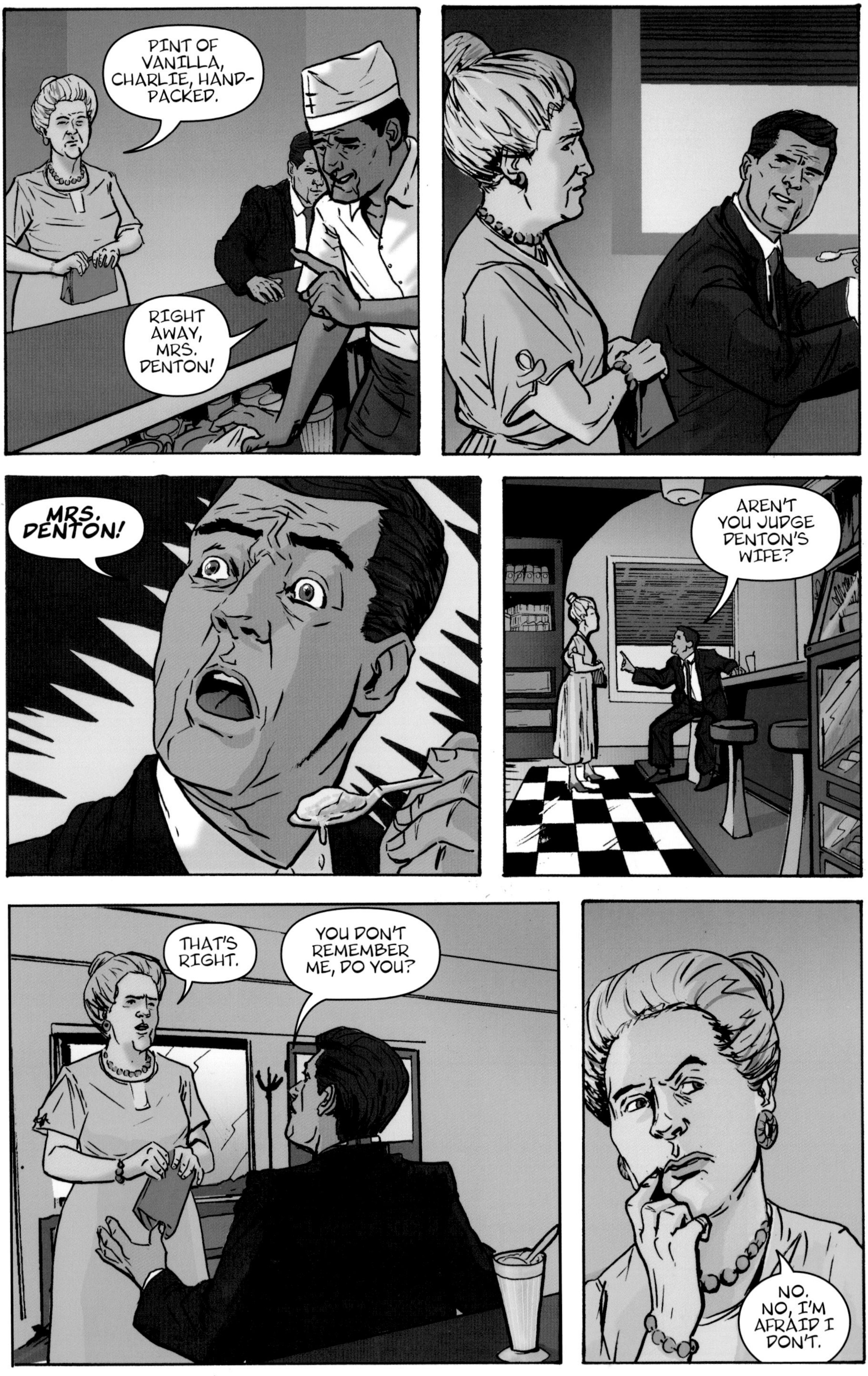
PINT OF VANILLA, CHARLIE, HAND-PACKED.
RIGHT AWAY, MRS. DENTON!
MRS. DENTON!
AREN'T YOU JUDGE DENTON'S WIFE?
THAT'S RIGHT.
YOU DON'T REMEMBER ME, DO YOU?
NO. NO, I'M AFRAID I DON'T.

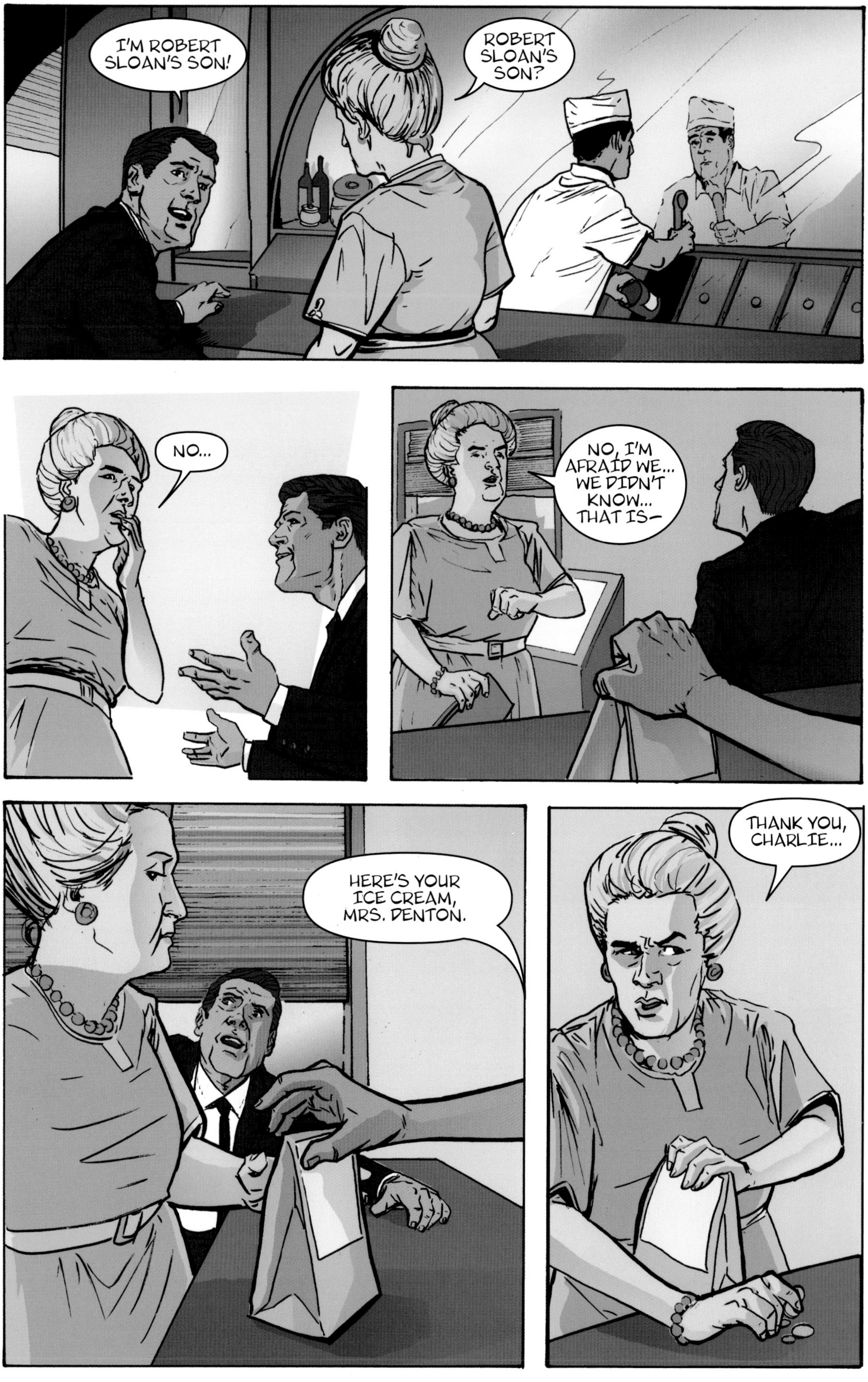
I'M ROBERT SLOAN'S SON!
ROBERT SLOAN'S SON?
NO...
NO, I'M AFRAID WE... WE DIDN'T KNOW... THAT IS—
HERE'S YOUR ICE CREAM, MRS. DENTON.
THANK YOU, CHARLIE...

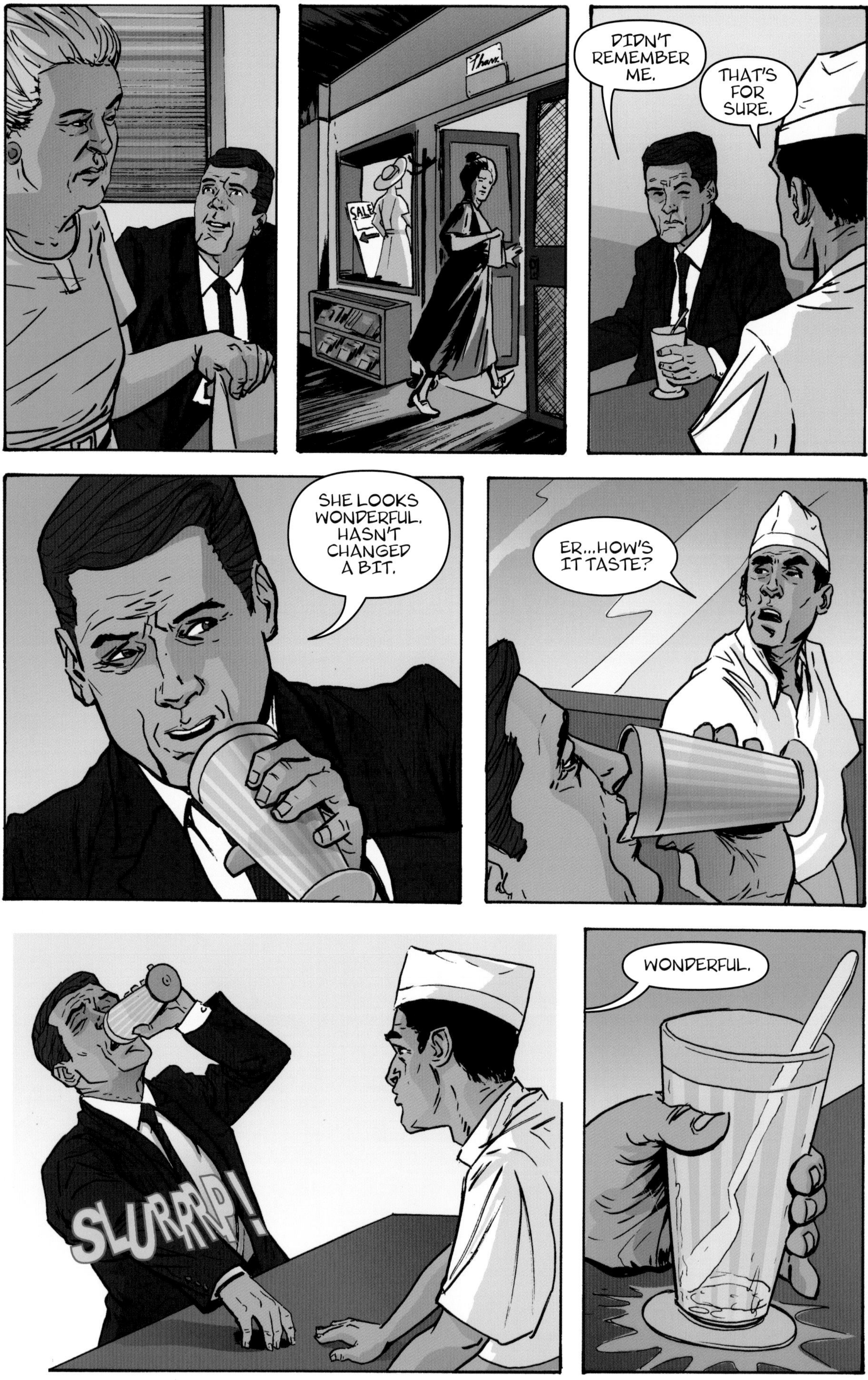
SALE
DIDN'T REMEMBER ME.
THAT'S FOR SURE.
SHE LOOKS WONDERFUL. HASN'T CHANGED A BIT.
ER...HOW'S IT TASTE?
SLURRRP!
WONDERFUL.

FUNNY. I ALWAYS THOUGHT THAT...

...IF I EVER CAME BACK HERE...THE PLACE WOULD PROBABLY BE ALL CHANGED.

I GUESS YOU ALWAYS THINK ABOUT YOUR HOMETOWN. YOU KNOW...

...YOU BUILD UP IMAGES OF IT IN YOUR MIND. QUIET STREETS, TREES ALL OVER. THEN YOU COME BACK AND...

...IT'S GROWN UP WITH YOU AND IT DOESN'T TAKE THE CHANGE VERY WELL.

BUT NOT THIS PLACE. IT'S JUST AS IF...JUST AS IF I LEFT YESTERDAY.

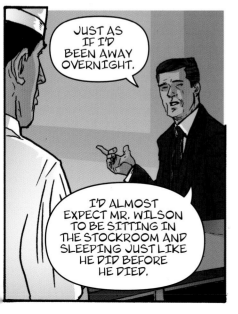

JUST AS IF I'D BEEN AWAY OVERNIGHT.

I'D ALMOST EXPECT MR. WILSON TO BE SITTING IN THE STOCKROOM AND SLEEPING JUST LIKE HE DID BEFORE HE DIED.

THAT'S ONE OF THE IMAGES I HAVE. OLD MAN WILSON SLEEPING IN HIS BIG COMFORTABLE CHAIR UP THERE. IT DOESN'T TAKE A COMMITTEE TO RUN THIS PLACE...

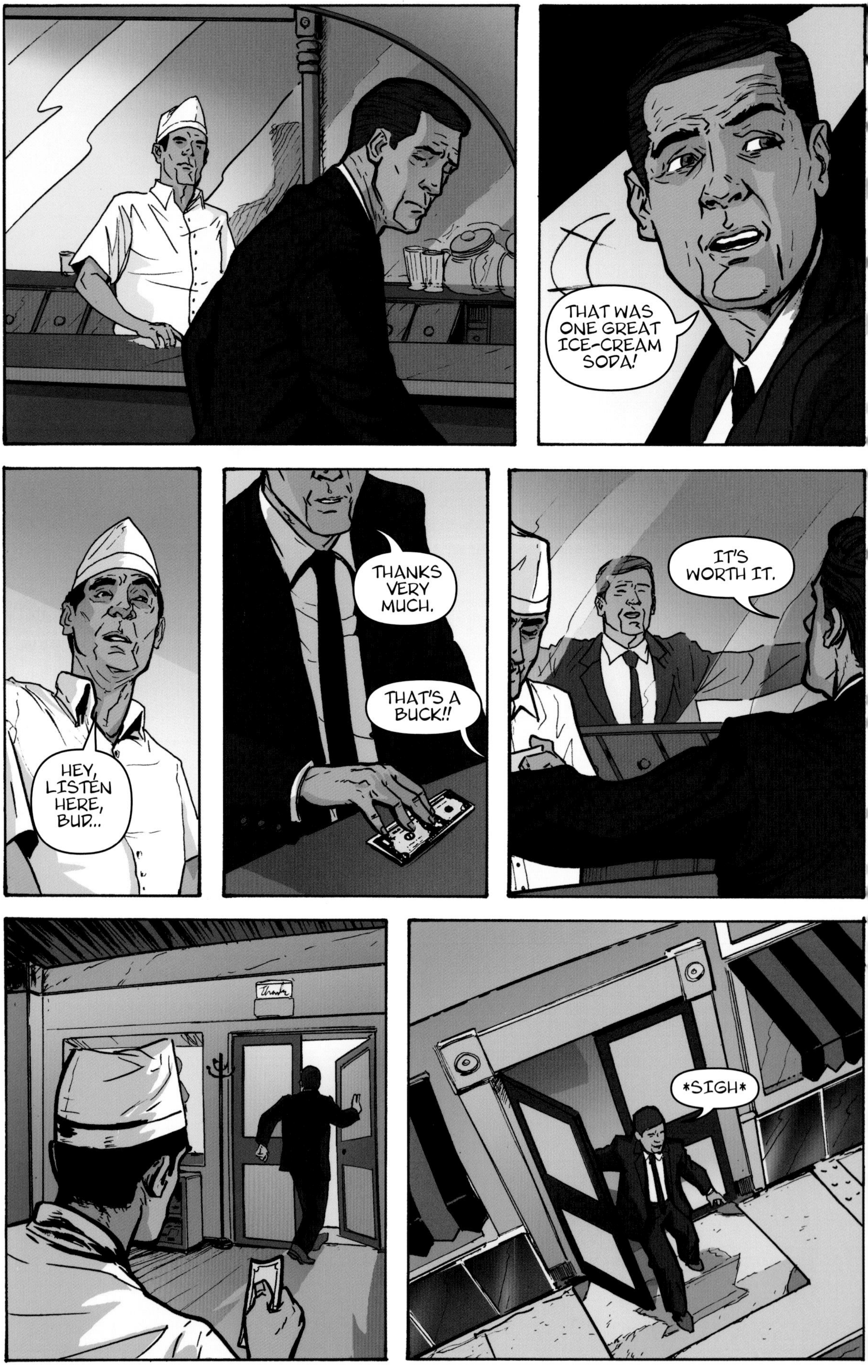
THAT WAS ONE GREAT ICE-CREAM SODA!
HEY, LISTEN HERE, BUD...
THANKS VERY MUCH.
THAT'S A BUCK!!
IT'S WORTH IT.
SIGH

WE'RE GONNA NEED SOME MORE CHOCOLATE SYRUP, MR. WILSON.

MR. WILSON?

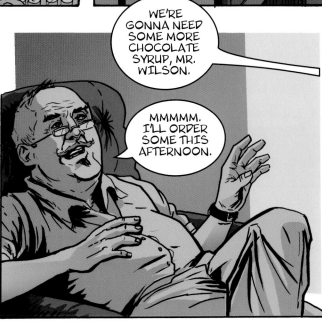

MMMMM, I'LL ORDER SOME THIS AFTERNOON.

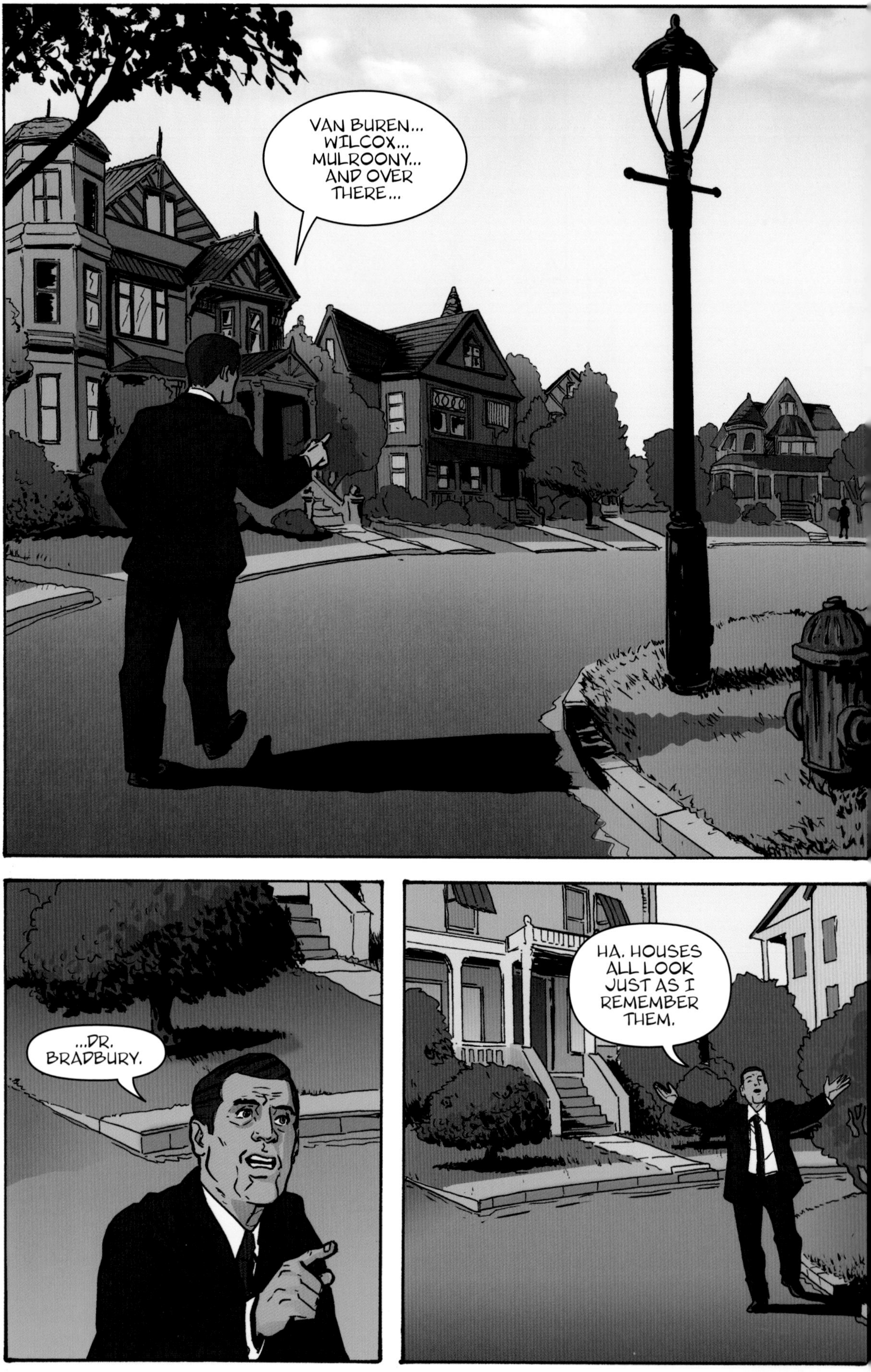
VAN BUREN... WILCOX... MULROONY... AND OVER THERE...
...DR. BRADBURY.
HA. HOUSES ALL LOOK JUST AS I REMEMBER THEM.

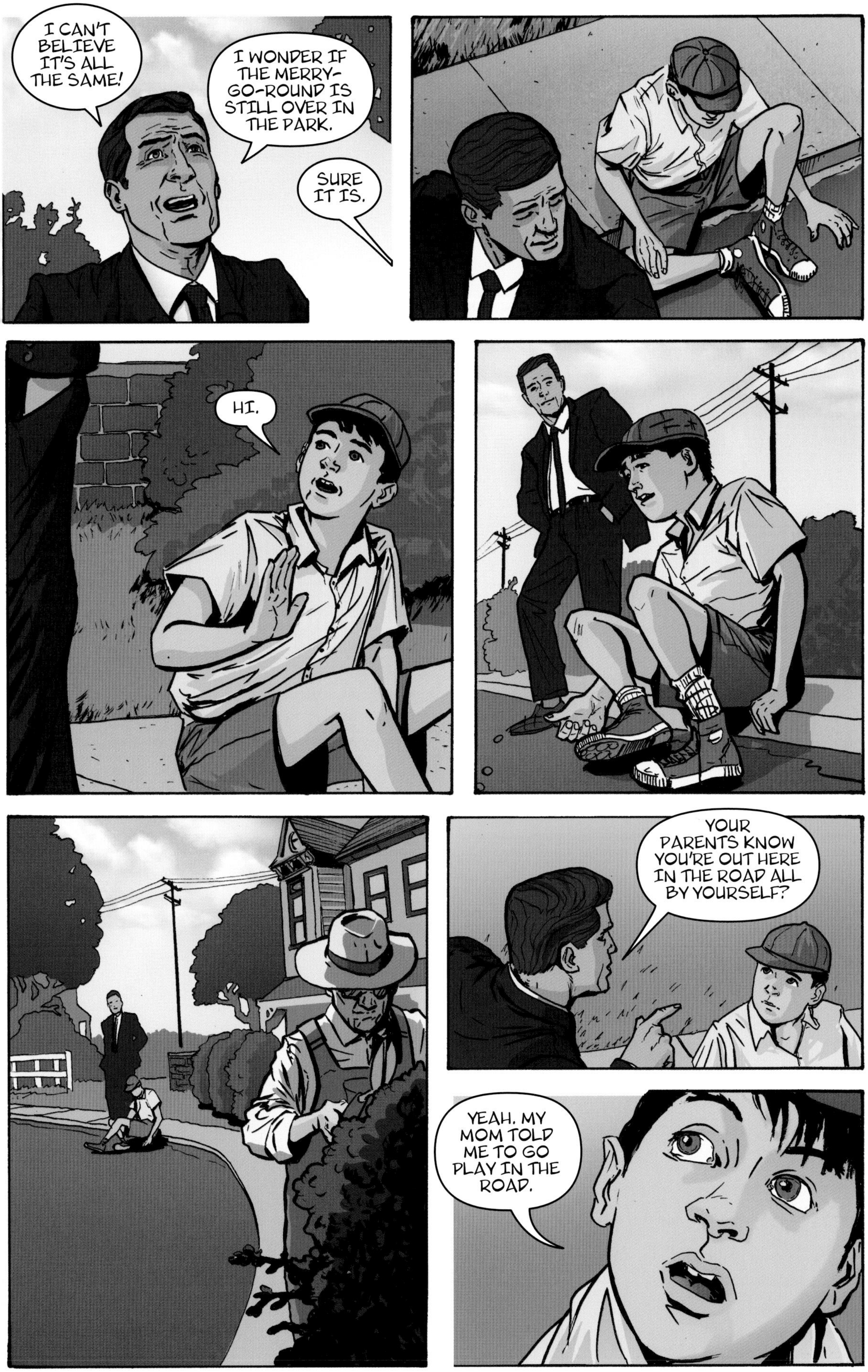
I CAN'T BELIEVE IT'S ALL THE SAME!
I WONDER IF THE MERRY-GO-ROUND IS STILL OVER IN THE PARK.
SURE IT IS.
HI.
YOUR PARENTS KNOW YOU'RE OUT HERE IN THE ROAD ALL BY YOURSELF?
YEAH. MY MOM TOLD ME TO GO PLAY IN THE ROAD.

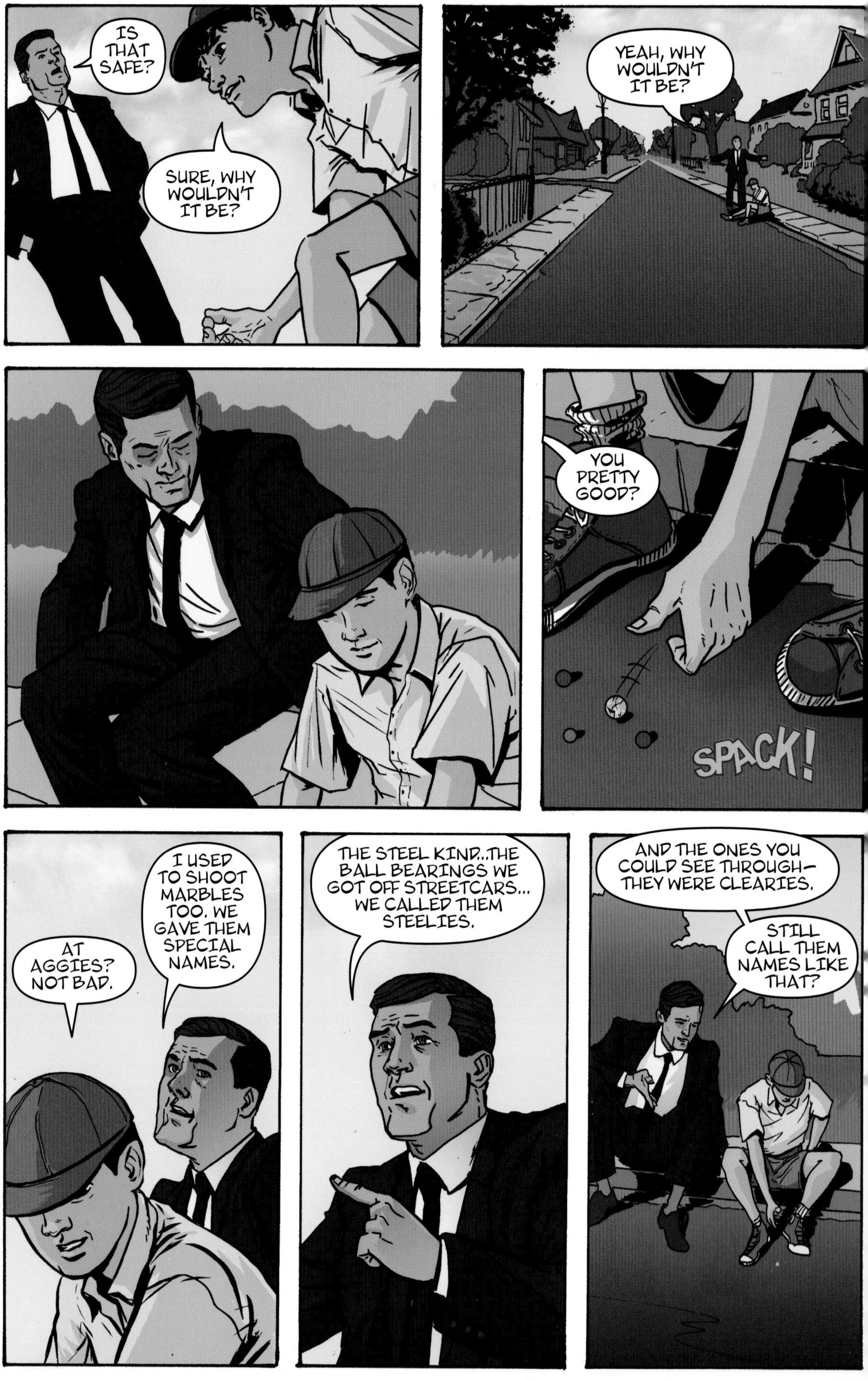
IS THAT SAFE?
SURE, WHY WOULDN'T IT BE?
YEAH, WHY WOULDN'T IT BE?
YOU PRETTY GOOD?
SPACK!
AT AGGIES? NOT BAD.
I USED TO SHOOT MARBLES TOO. WE GAVE THEM SPECIAL NAMES.
THE STEEL KIND...THE BALL BEARINGS WE GOT OFF STREETCARS... WE CALLED THEM STEELIES.
AND THE ONES YOU COULD SEE THROUGH— THEY WERE CLEARIES.
STILL CALL THEM NAMES LIKE THAT?

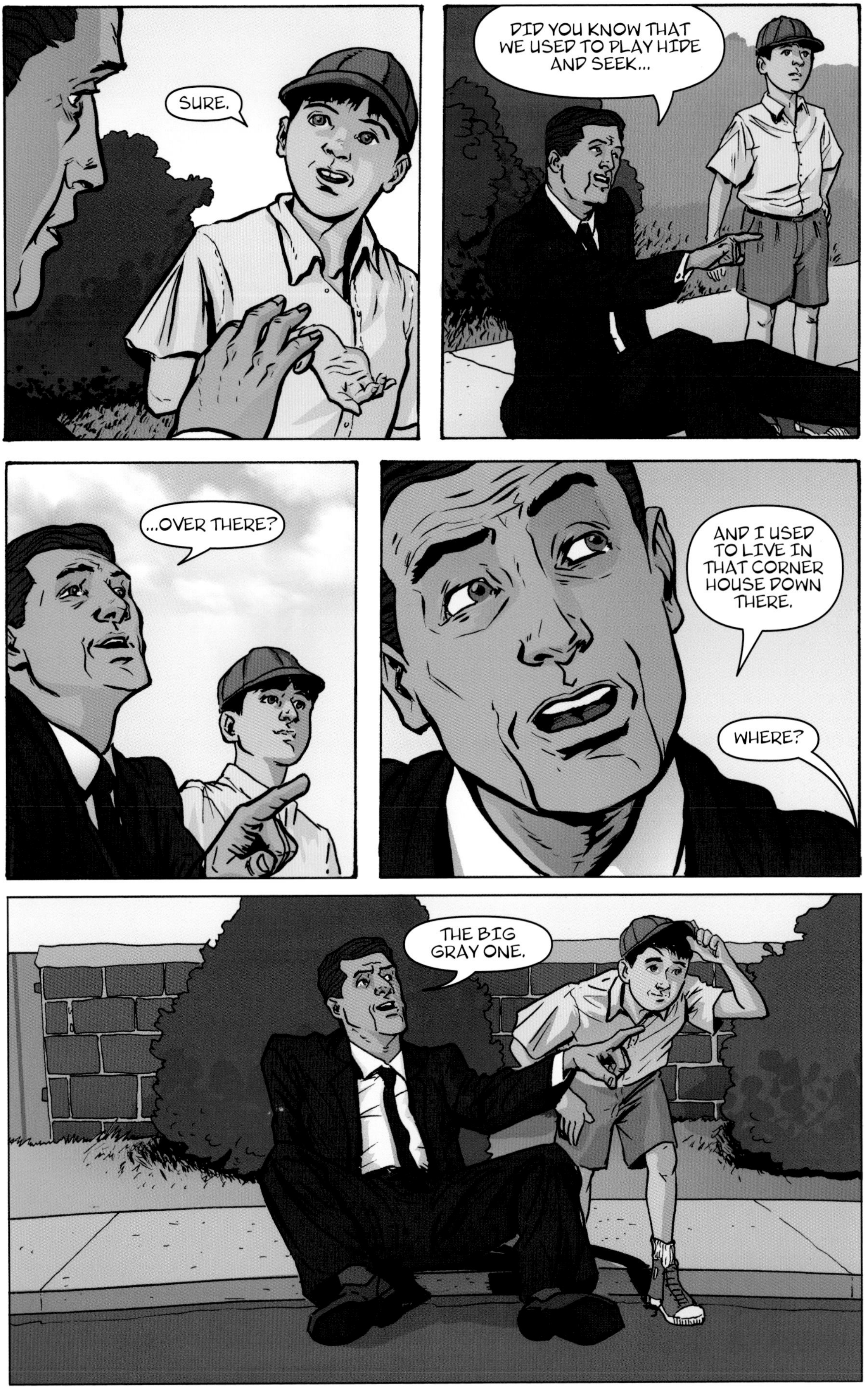
SURE.
DID YOU KNOW THAT WE USED TO PLAY HIDE AND SEEK...
...OVER THERE?
AND I USED TO LIVE IN THAT CORNER HOUSE DOWN THERE.
WHERE?
THE BIG GRAY ONE.

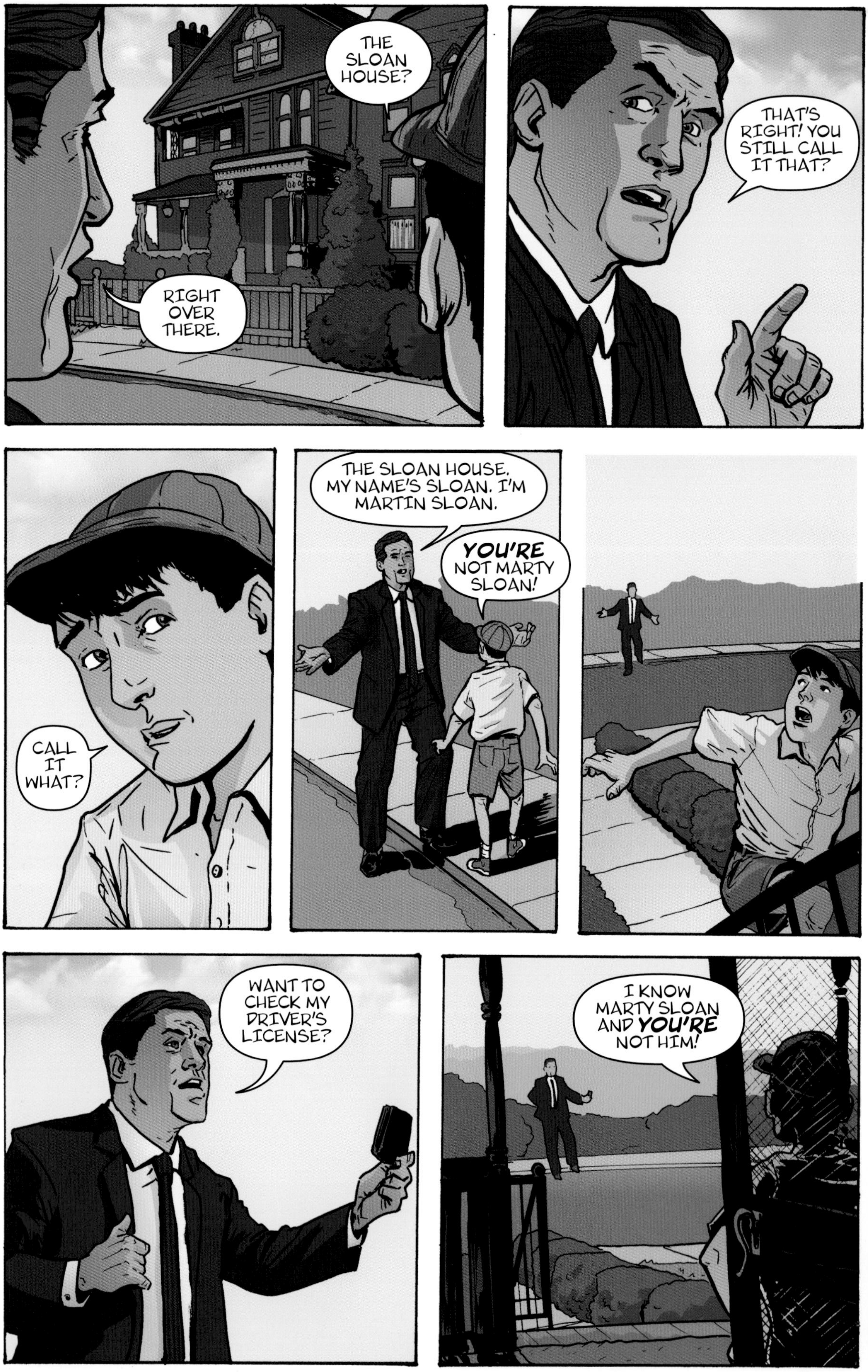
THE SLOAN HOUSE?
RIGHT OVER THERE.
THAT'S RIGHT! YOU STILL CALL IT THAT?
CALL IT WHAT?
THE SLOAN HOUSE. MY NAME'S SLOAN. I'M MARTIN SLOAN.
YOU'RE NOT MARTY SLOAN!
WANT TO CHECK MY DRIVER'S LICENSE?
I KNOW MARTY SLOAN AND YOU'RE NOT HIM!

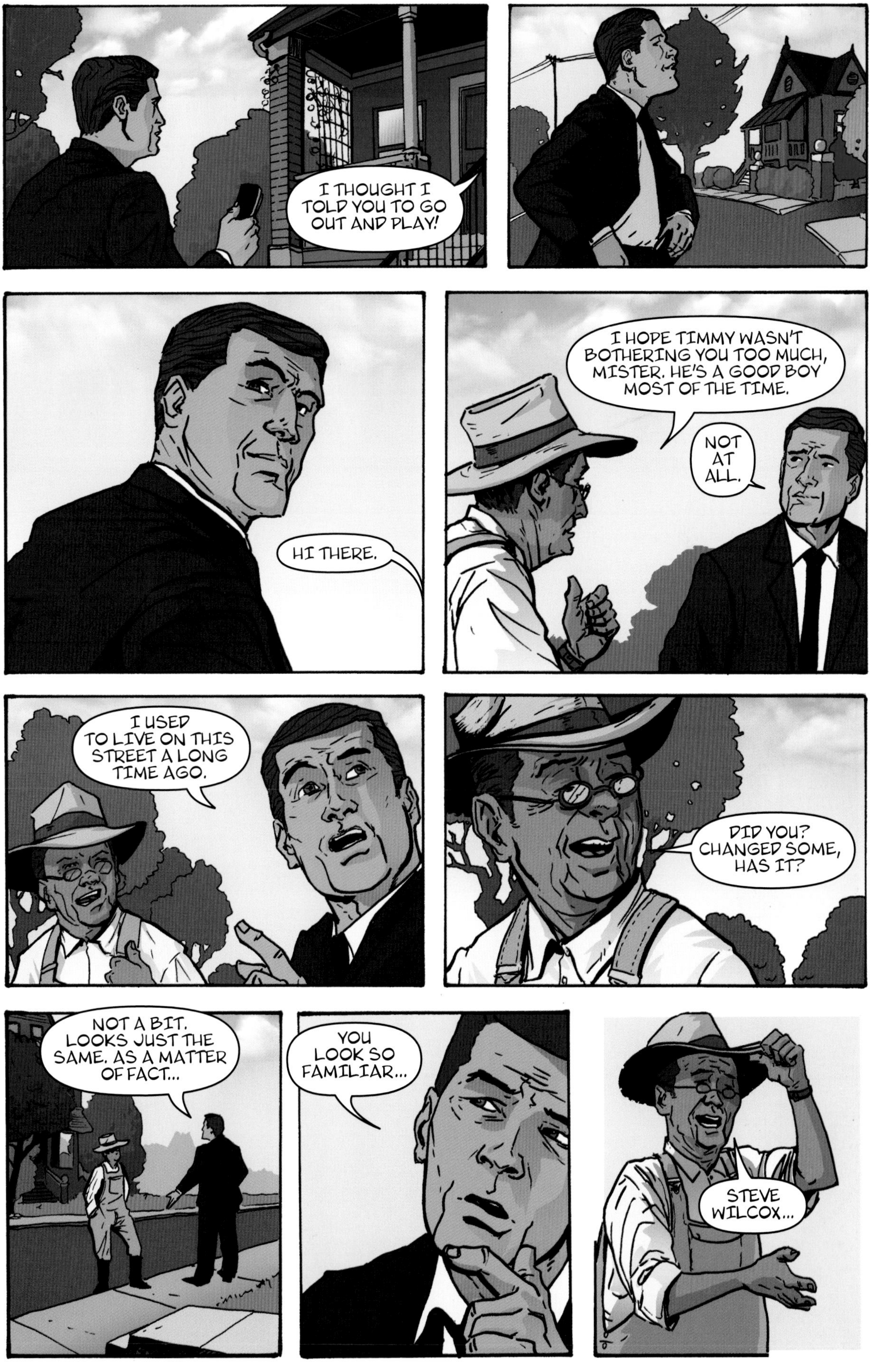
I THOUGHT I TOLD YOU TO GO OUT AND PLAY!
HI THERE.
I HOPE TIMMY WASN'T BOTHERING YOU TOO MUCH, MISTER. HE'S A GOOD BOY MOST OF THE TIME.
NOT AT ALL.
I USED TO LIVE ON THIS STREET A LONG TIME AGO.
DID YOU? CHANGED SOME, HAS IT?
NOT A BIT. LOOKS JUST THE SAME. AS A MATTER OF FACT...
YOU LOOK SO FAMILIAR...
STEVE WILCOX...

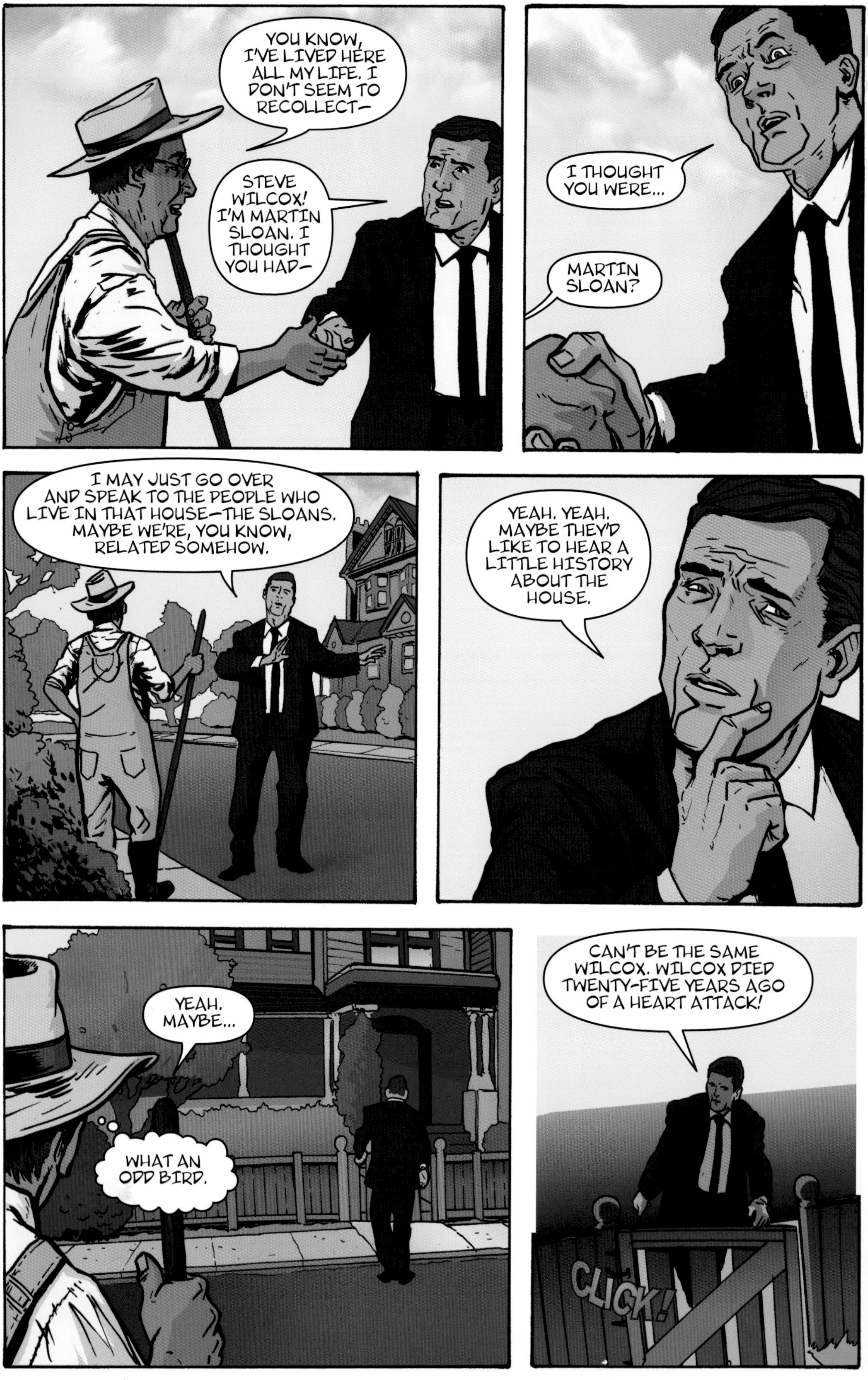
YOU KNOW, I'VE LIVED HERE ALL MY LIFE. I DON'T SEEM TO RECOLLECT—
STEVE WILCOX! I'M MARTIN SLOAN. I THOUGHT YOU HAD—
I THOUGHT YOU WERE...
MARTIN SLOAN?
I MAY JUST GO OVER AND SPEAK TO THE PEOPLE WHO LIVE IN THAT HOUSE—THE SLOANS. MAYBE WE'RE, YOU KNOW, RELATED SOMEHOW.
YEAH. YEAH. MAYBE THEY'D LIKE TO HEAR A LITTLE HISTORY ABOUT THE HOUSE.
YEAH. MAYBE...
WHAT AN ODD BIRD.
CAN'T BE THE SAME WILCOX. WILCOX DIED TWENTY-FIVE YEARS AGO OF A HEART ATTACK!
CLICK!

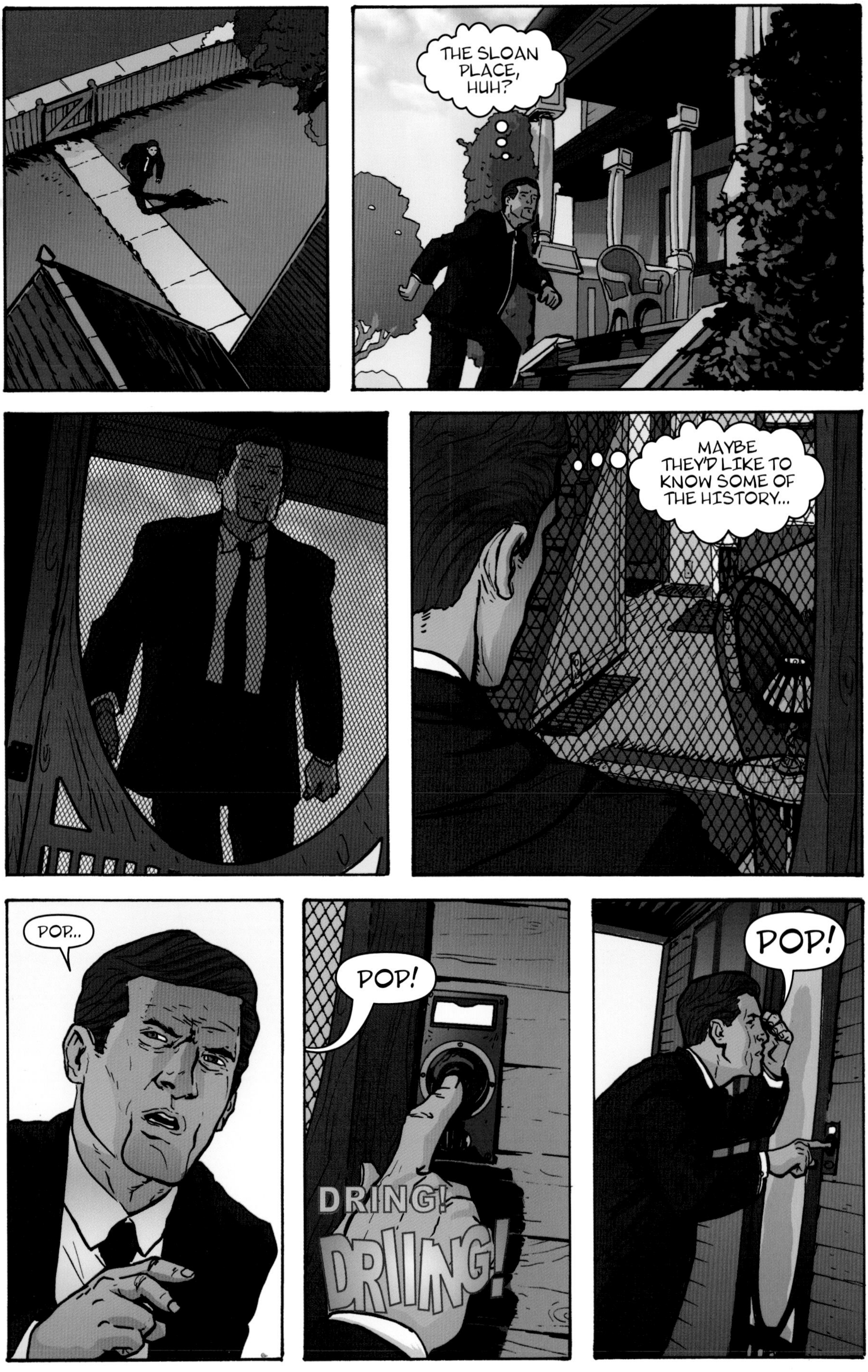
THE SLOAN PLACE, HUH?
MAYBE THEY'D LIKE TO KNOW SOME OF THE HISTORY...
POP...
POP!
DRING!
DRIIING!
POP!

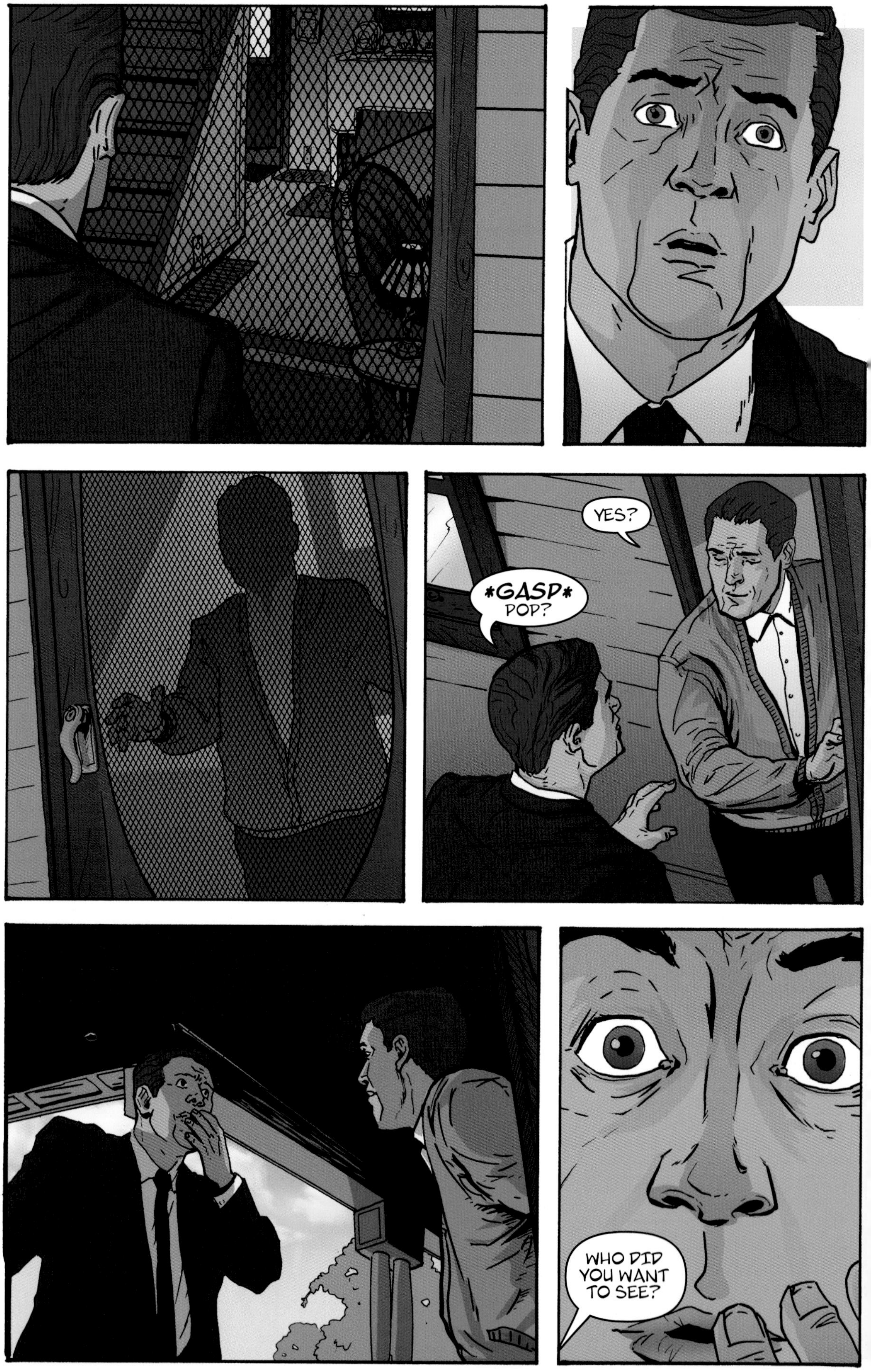
YES?
GASP POP?
WHO DID YOU WANT TO SEE?

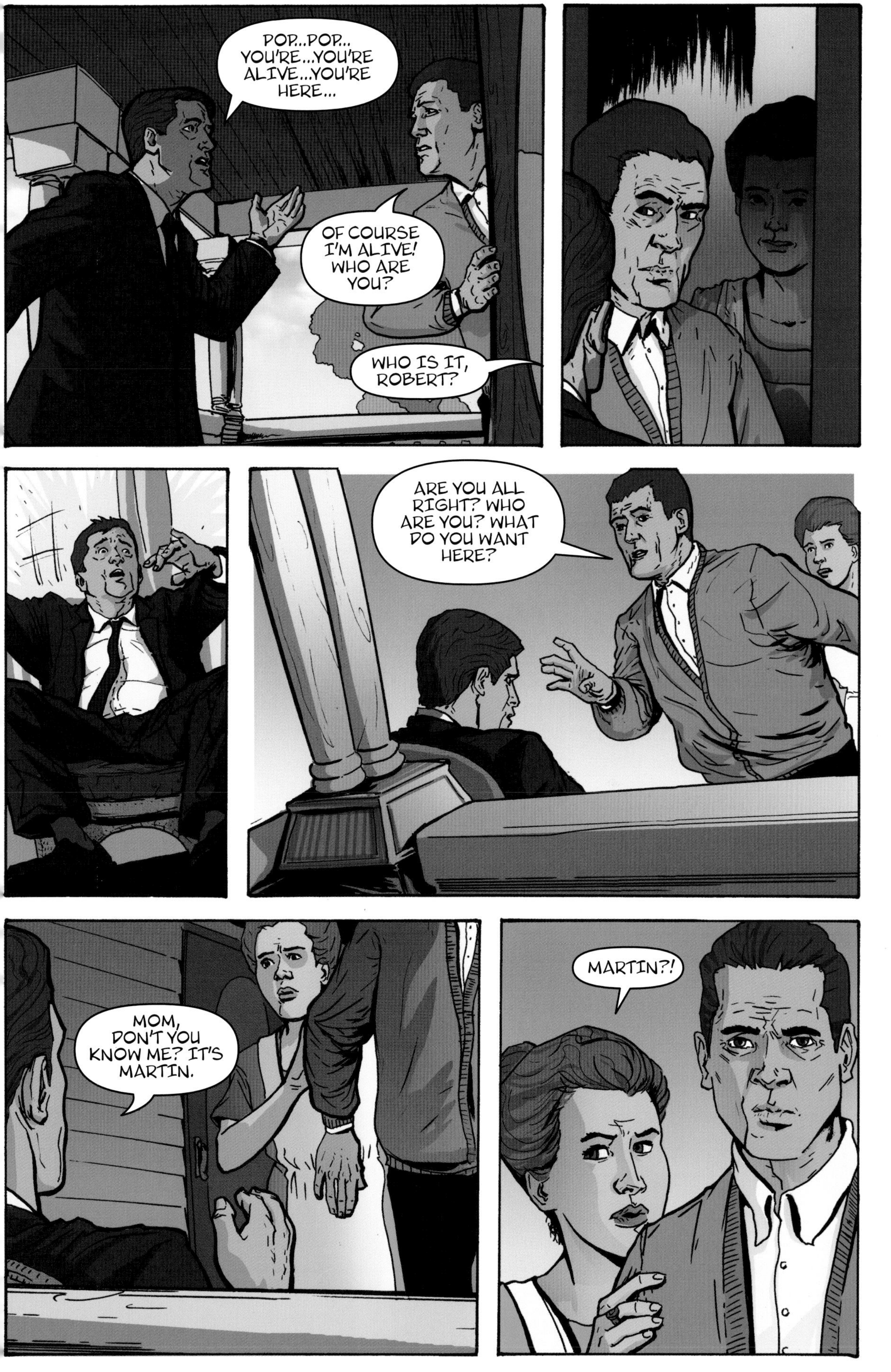
POP...POP... YOU'RE...YOU'RE ALIVE...YOU'RE HERE...
OF COURSE I'M ALIVE! WHO ARE YOU?
WHO IS IT, ROBERT?
ARE YOU ALL RIGHT? WHO ARE YOU? WHAT DO YOU WANT HERE?
MOM, DON'T YOU KNOW ME? IT'S MARTIN.
MARTIN?!

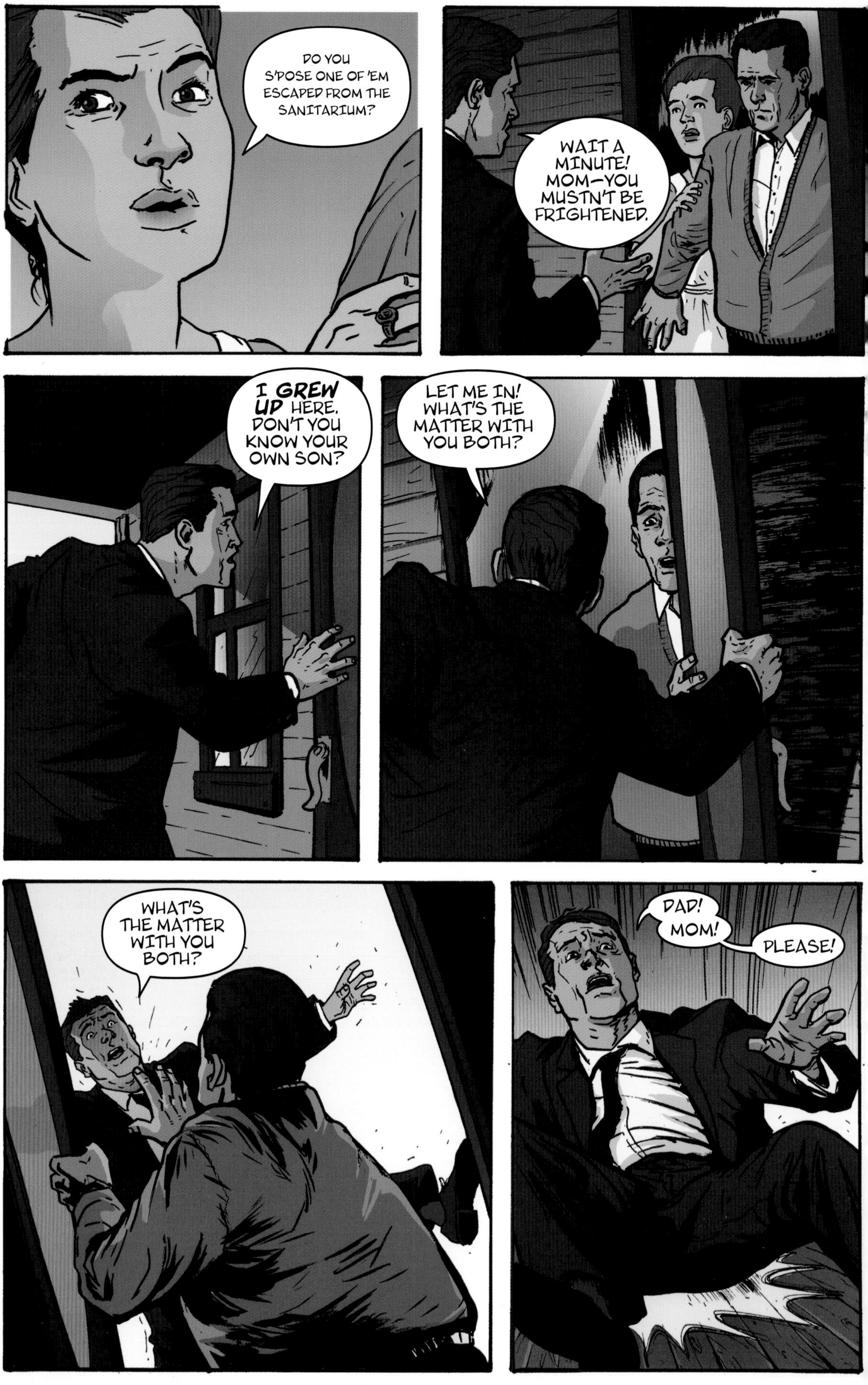
DO YOU S'POSE ONE OF 'EM ESCAPED FROM THE SANITARIUM?
WAIT A MINUTE! MOM—YOU MUSTN'T BE FRIGHTENED.
I GREW UP HERE. DON'T YOU KNOW YOUR OWN SON?
LET ME IN! WHAT'S THE MATTER WITH YOU BOTH?
WHAT'S THE MATTER WITH YOU BOTH?
DAD!
MOM!
PLEASE!

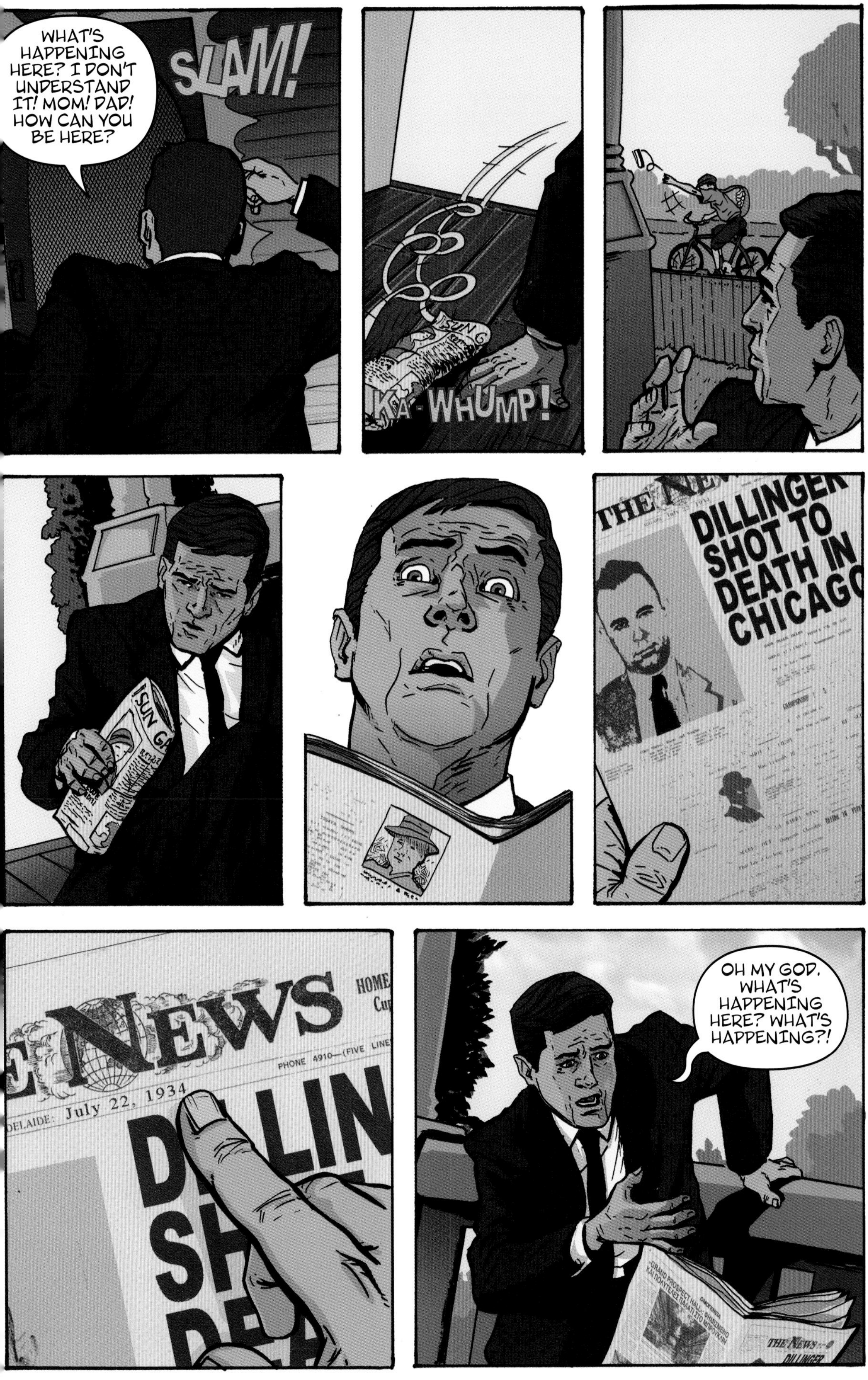
WHAT'S HAPPENING HERE? I DON'T UNDERSTAND IT! MOM! DAD! HOW CAN YOU BE HERE?
SLAM!
KA-WHUMP!
DILLINGER SHOT TO DEATH IN CHICAGO
July 22, 1934
OH MY GOD. WHAT'S HAPPENING HERE? WHAT'S HAPPENING?!

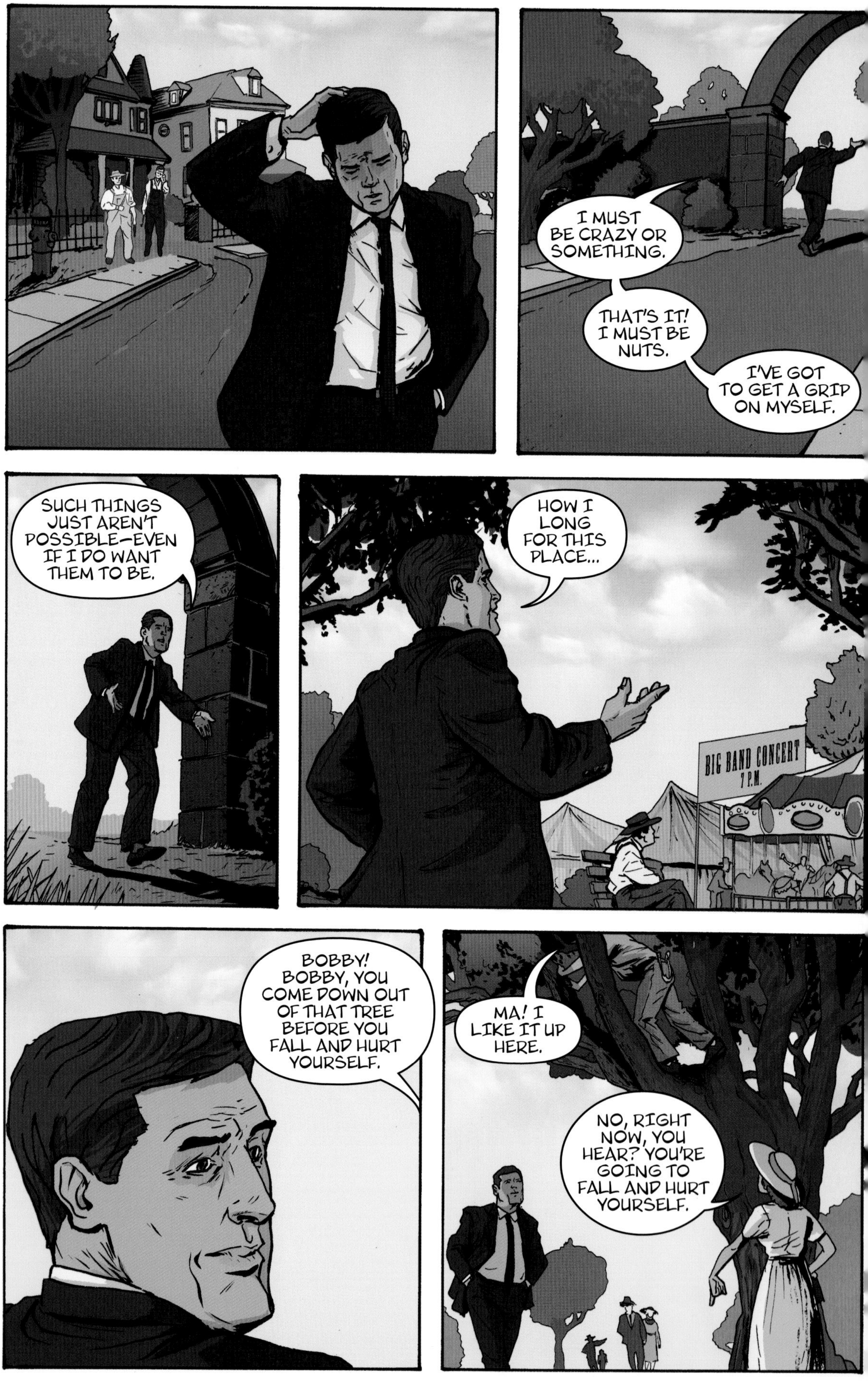
I MUST BE CRAZY OR SOMETHING.
THAT'S IT! I MUST BE NUTS.
I'VE GOT TO GET A GRIP ON MYSELF.
SUCH THINGS JUST AREN'T POSSIBLE—EVEN IF I DO WANT THEM TO BE.
HOW I LONG FOR THIS PLACE...
BIG BAND CONCERT 7 P.M.
BOBBY! BOBBY, YOU COME DOWN OUT OF THAT TREE BEFORE YOU FALL AND HURT YOURSELF.
MA! I LIKE IT UP HERE.
NO, RIGHT NOW, YOU HEAR? YOU'RE GOING TO FALL AND HURT YOURSELF.

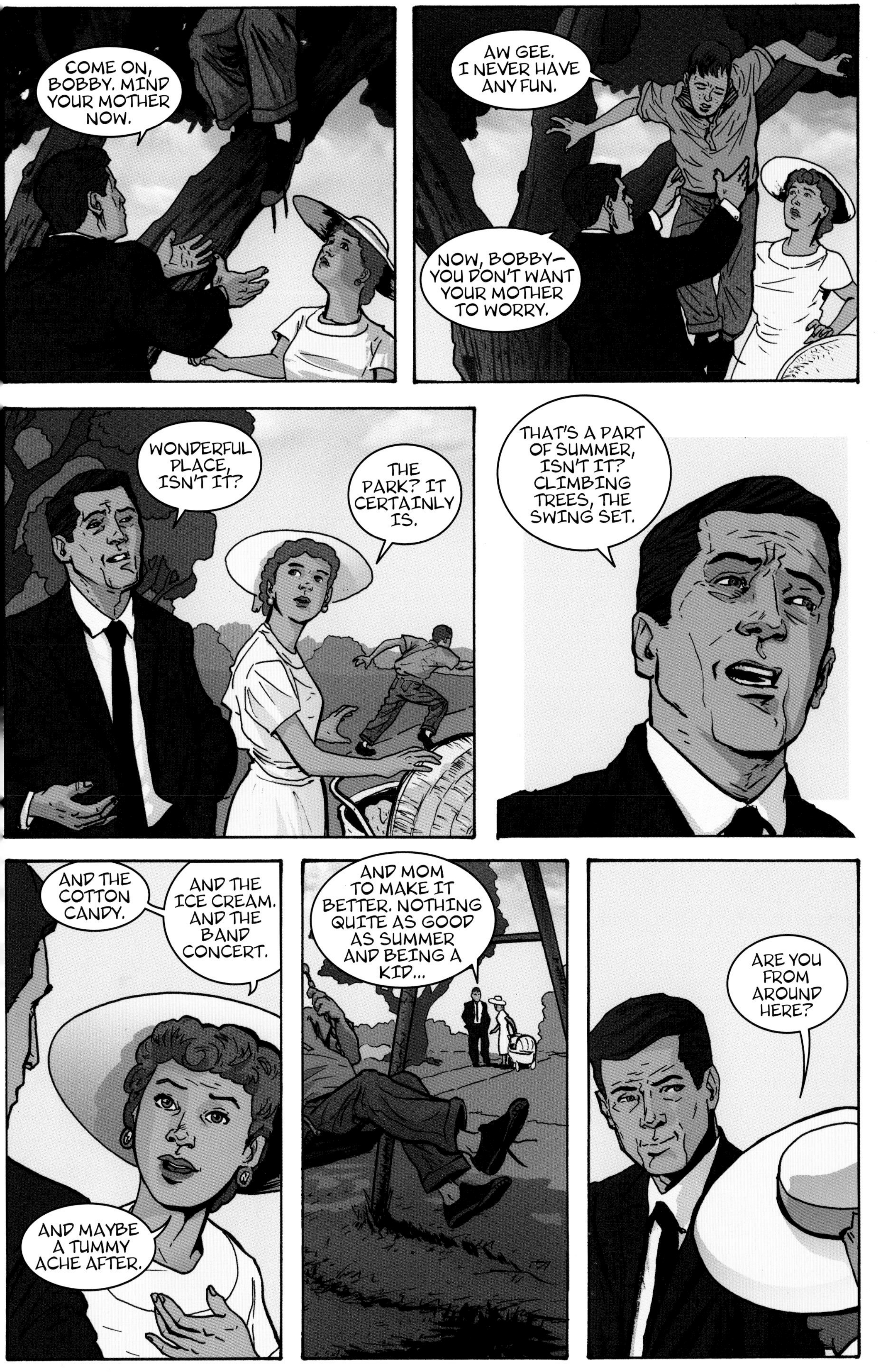
COME ON, BOBBY. MIND YOUR MOTHER NOW.
AW GEE. I NEVER HAVE ANY FUN.
NOW, BOBBY– YOU DON'T WANT YOUR MOTHER TO WORRY.
WONDERFUL PLACE, ISN'T IT?
THE PARK? IT CERTAINLY IS.
THAT'S A PART OF SUMMER, ISN'T IT? CLIMBING TREES, THE SWING SET.
AND THE COTTON CANDY.
AND THE ICE CREAM. AND THE BAND CONCERT.
AND MAYBE A TUMMY ACHE AFTER.
AND MOM TO MAKE IT BETTER. NOTHING QUITE AS GOOD AS SUMMER AND BEING A KID...
ARE YOU FROM AROUND HERE?

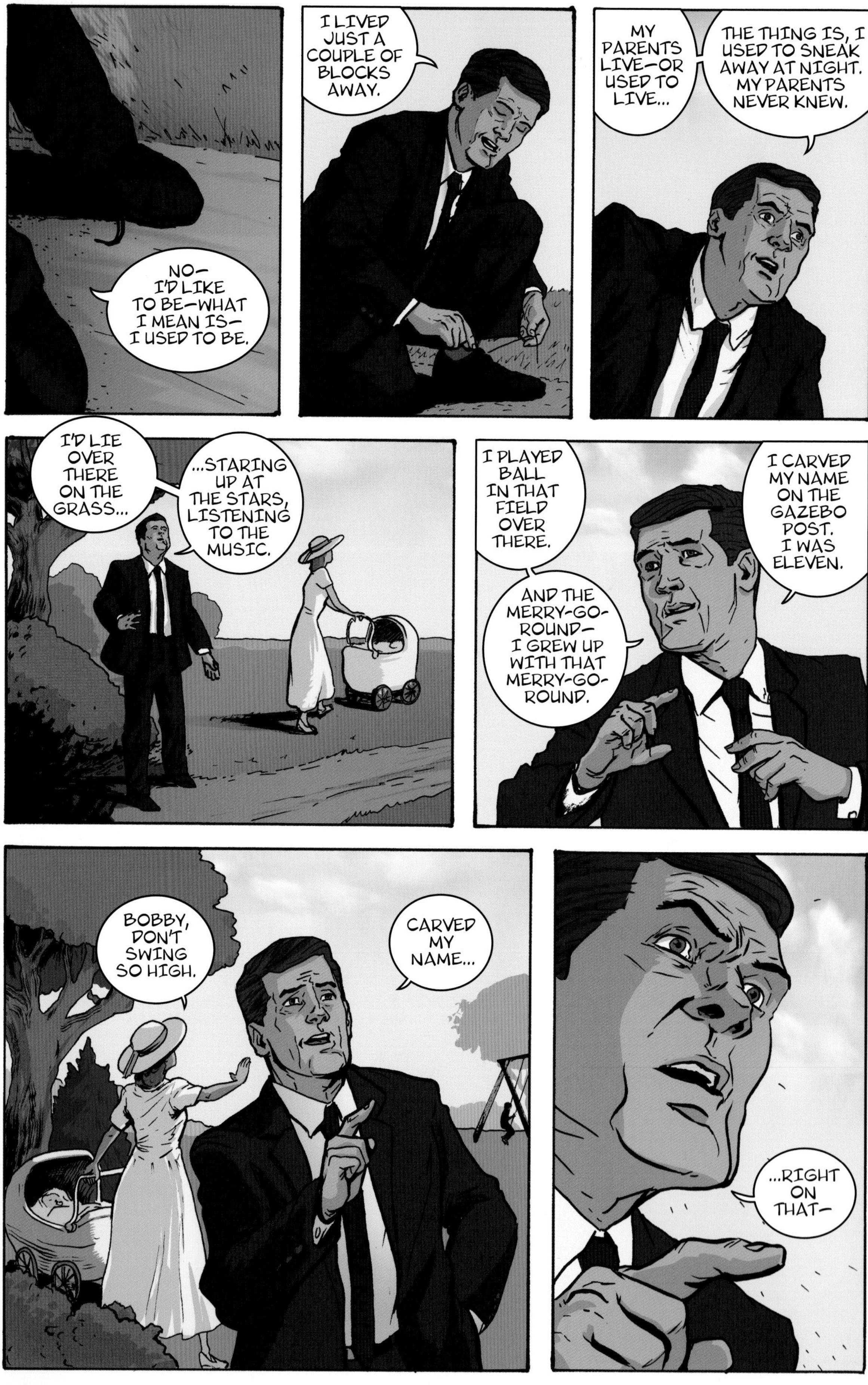
NO— I'D LIKE TO BE—WHAT I MEAN IS— I USED TO BE.
I LIVED JUST A COUPLE OF BLOCKS AWAY.
MY PARENTS LIVE—OR USED TO LIVE...
THE THING IS, I USED TO SNEAK AWAY AT NIGHT. MY PARENTS NEVER KNEW.
I'D LIE OVER THERE ON THE GRASS...
...STARING UP AT THE STARS, LISTENING TO THE MUSIC.
I PLAYED BALL IN THAT FIELD OVER THERE.
AND THE MERRY-GO-ROUND— I GREW UP WITH THAT MERRY-GO-ROUND.
I CARVED MY NAME ON THE GAZEBO POST. I WAS ELEVEN.
BOBBY, DON'T SWING SO HIGH.
CARVED MY NAME...
...RIGHT ON THAT—

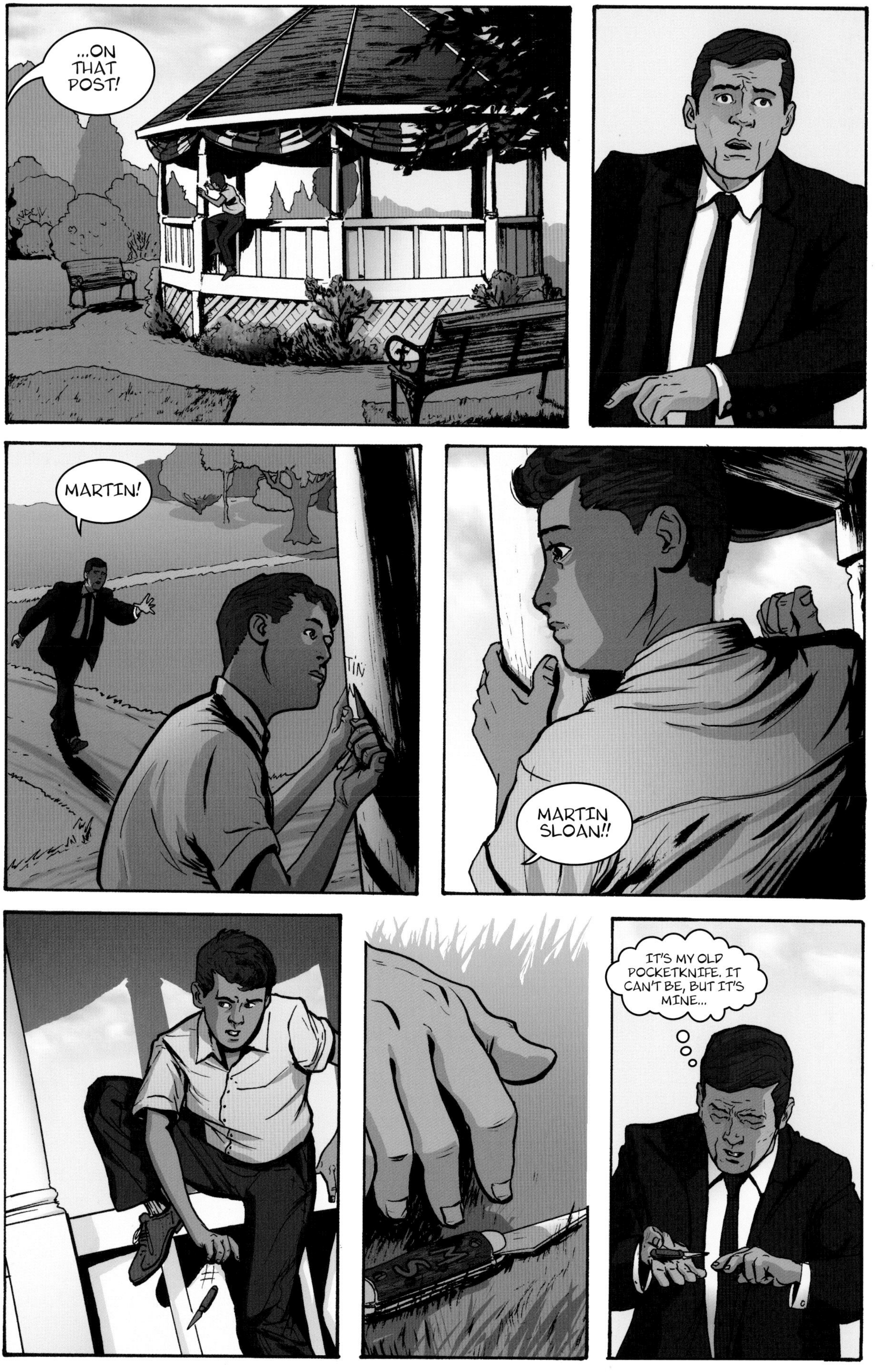
...ON THAT POST!
MARTIN!
MARTIN SLOAN!!
IT'S MY OLD POCKETKNIFE. IT CAN'T BE, BUT IT'S MINE...

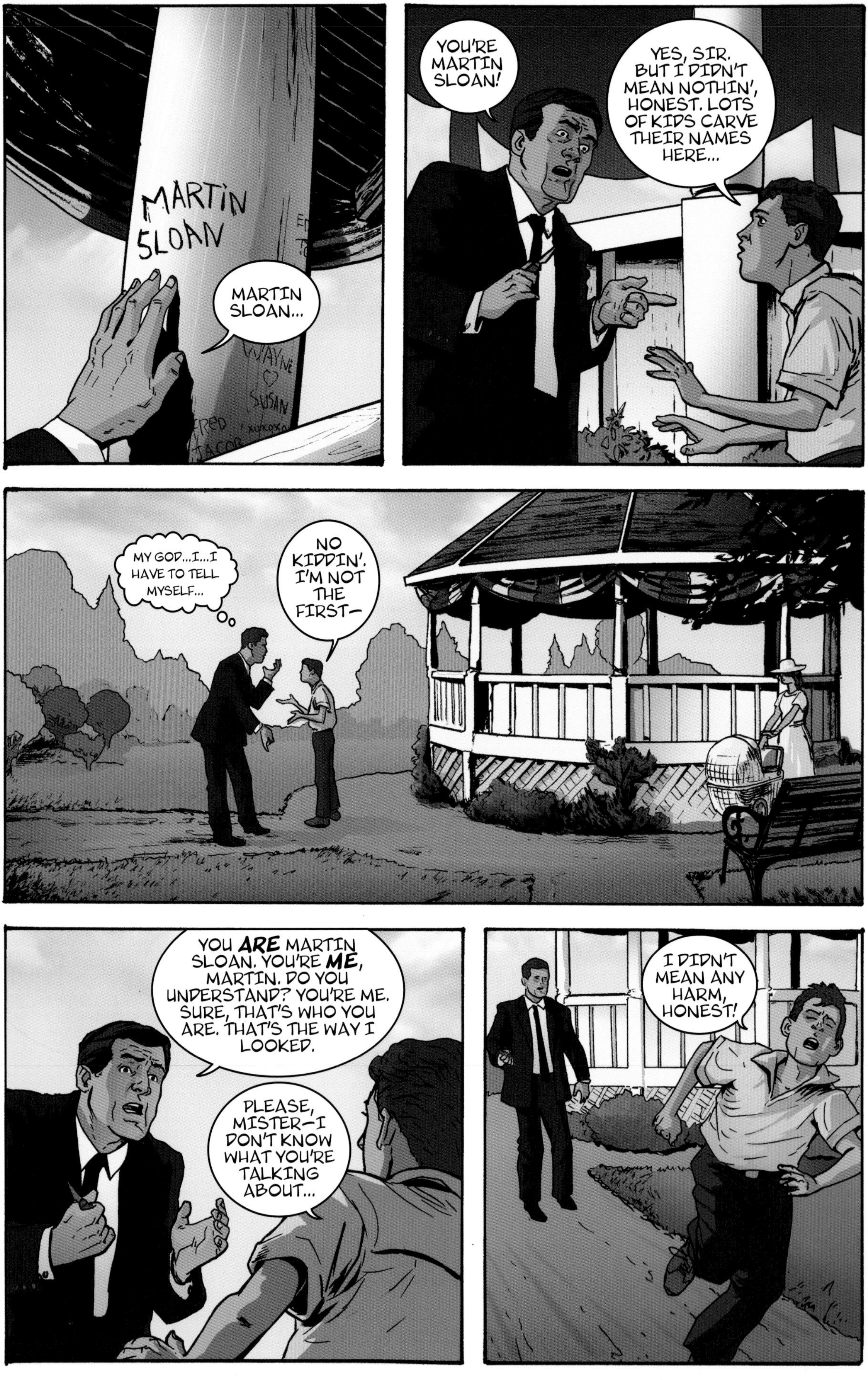
MARTIN SLOAN
WAYNE ♥ SUSAN
MARTIN SLOAN...
YOU'RE MARTIN SLOAN!
YES, SIR. BUT I DIDN'T MEAN NOTHIN', HONEST. LOTS OF KIDS CARVE THEIR NAMES HERE...
MY GOD...I...I HAVE TO TELL MYSELF...
NO KIDDIN'. I'M NOT THE FIRST—
YOU **ARE** MARTIN SLOAN. YOU'RE **ME**, MARTIN. DO YOU UNDERSTAND? YOU'RE ME. SURE, THAT'S WHO YOU ARE. THAT'S THE WAY I LOOKED.
PLEASE, MISTER—I DON'T KNOW WHAT YOU'RE TALKING ABOUT...
I DIDN'T MEAN ANY HARM, HONEST!

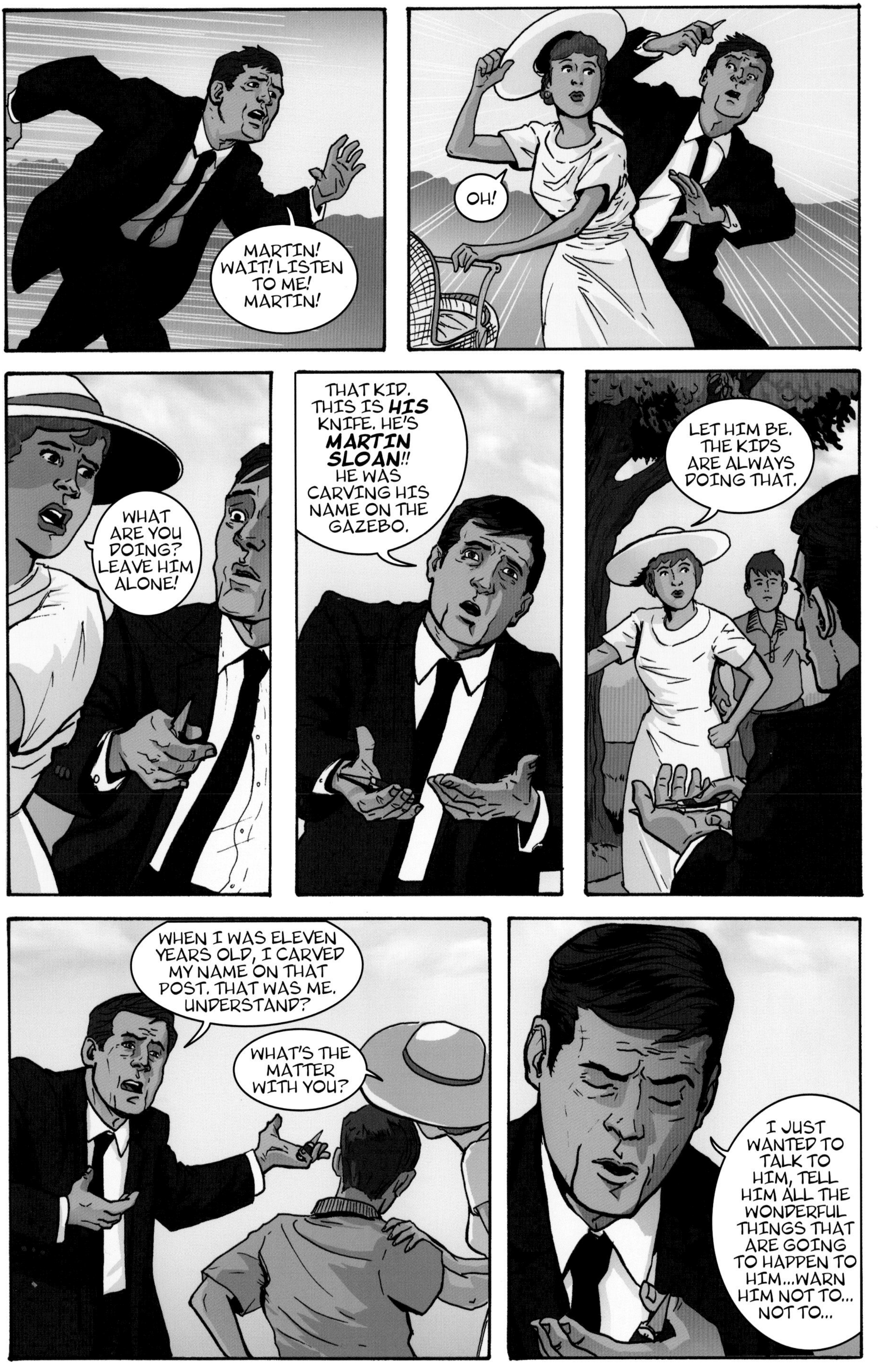
MARTIN! WAIT! LISTEN TO ME! MARTIN!
OH!
WHAT ARE YOU DOING? LEAVE HIM ALONE!
THAT KID. THIS IS **HIS** KNIFE. HE'S **MARTIN SLOAN**!! HE WAS CARVING HIS NAME ON THE GAZEBO.
LET HIM BE. THE KIDS ARE ALWAYS DOING THAT.
WHEN I WAS ELEVEN YEARS OLD, I CARVED MY NAME ON THAT POST. THAT WAS ME. UNDERSTAND?
WHAT'S THE MATTER WITH YOU?
I JUST WANTED TO TALK TO HIM, TELL HIM ALL THE WONDERFUL THINGS THAT ARE GOING TO HAPPEN TO HIM...WARN HIM NOT TO... NOT TO...

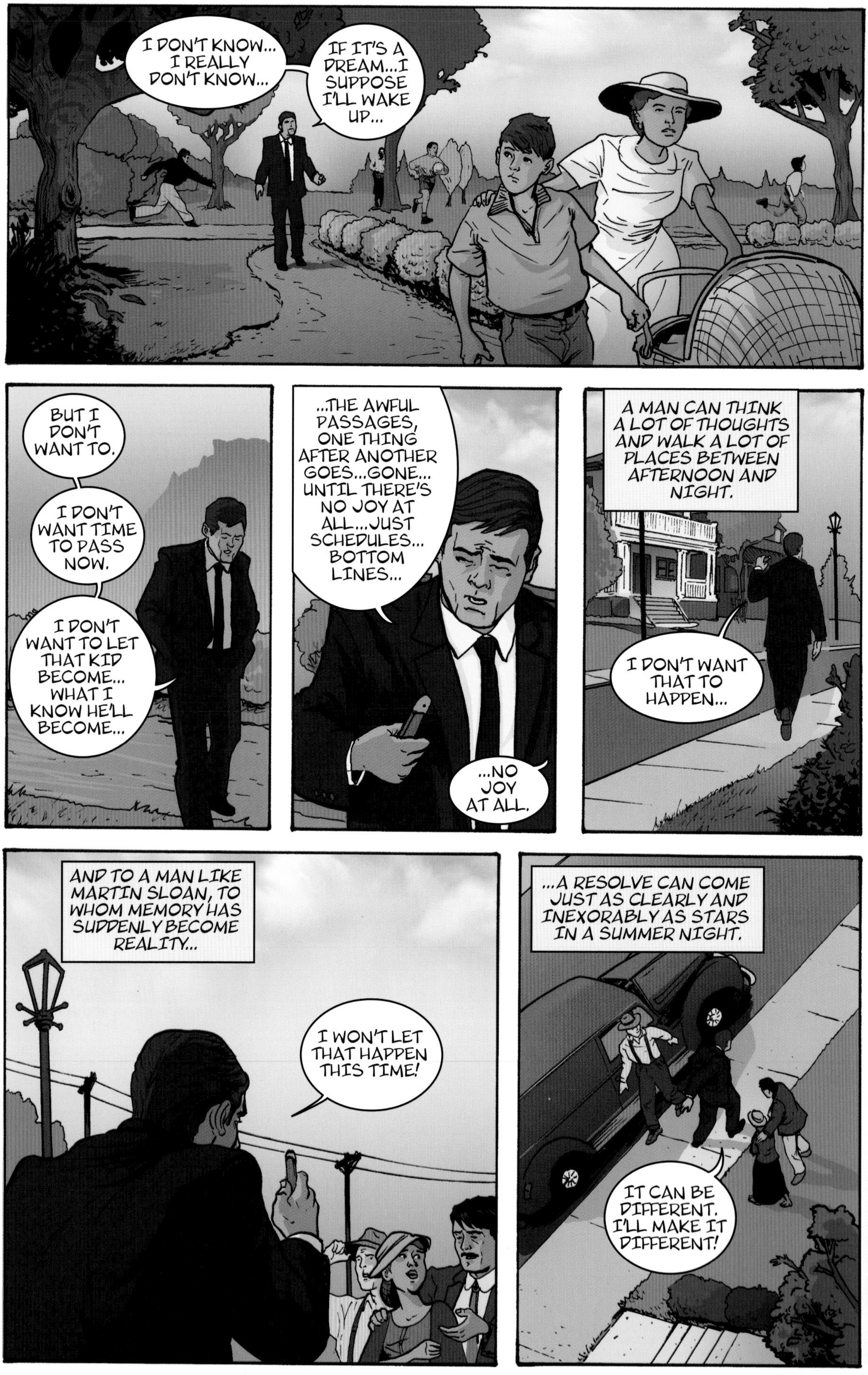
I DON'T KNOW... I REALLY DON'T KNOW...
IF IT'S A DREAM...I SUPPOSE I'LL WAKE UP...
BUT I DON'T WANT TO.
I DON'T WANT TIME TO PASS NOW.
I DON'T WANT TO LET THAT KID BECOME... WHAT I KNOW HE'LL BECOME...
...THE AWFUL PASSAGES, ONE THING AFTER ANOTHER GOES...GONE... UNTIL THERE'S NO JOY AT ALL...JUST SCHEDULES... BOTTOM LINES...
...NO JOY AT ALL.
A MAN CAN THINK A LOT OF THOUGHTS AND WALK A LOT OF PLACES BETWEEN AFTERNOON AND NIGHT.
I DON'T WANT THAT TO HAPPEN...
AND TO A MAN LIKE MARTIN SLOAN, TO WHOM MEMORY HAS SUDDENLY BECOME REALITY...
I WON'T LET THAT HAPPEN THIS TIME!
...A RESOLVE CAN COME JUST AS CLEARLY AND INEXORABLY AS STARS IN A SUMMER NIGHT.
IT CAN BE DIFFERENT. I'LL MAKE IT DIFFERENT!

MARTIN SLOAN IS NOW BACK IN TIME, AND HIS RESOLVE IS TO PUT IN A CLAIM—TO THE PAST.

CLICK!

YOU AGAIN? I HAD A FEELING YOU'D COME BACK.

I HAD TO COME BACK, POP—PLEASE DON'T SEND ME AWAY. I HAVE TO RETURN SOMETHING.

I HAVE TO GIVE IT BACK TO HIM, TO MARTIN. AND I HAVE TO TELL HIM—

WHERE'D YOU GET THAT? THAT'S MARTIN'S!

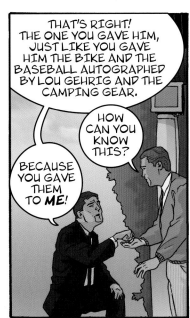

THAT'S RIGHT! THE ONE YOU GAVE HIM, JUST LIKE YOU GAVE HIM THE BIKE AND THE BASEBALL AUTOGRAPHED BY LOU GEHRIG AND THE CAMPING GEAR.

HOW CAN YOU KNOW THIS?

BECAUSE YOU GAVE THEM TO ME!

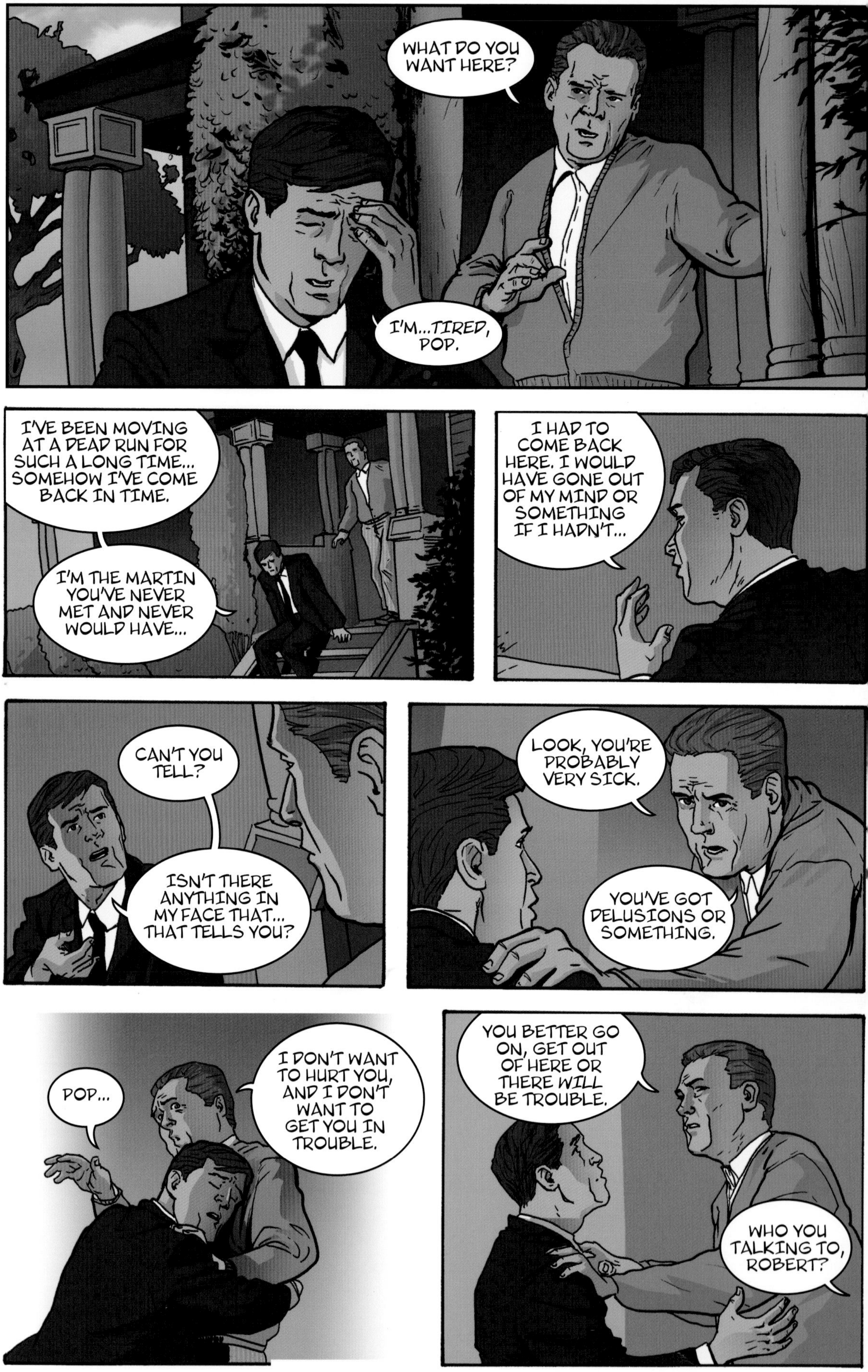
WHAT DO YOU WANT HERE?
I'M...TIRED, POP.
I'VE BEEN MOVING AT A DEAD RUN FOR SUCH A LONG TIME... SOMEHOW I'VE COME BACK IN TIME.
I'M THE MARTIN YOU'VE NEVER MET AND NEVER WOULD HAVE...
I HAD TO COME BACK HERE. I WOULD HAVE GONE OUT OF MY MIND OR SOMETHING IF I HADN'T...
CAN'T YOU TELL?
ISN'T THERE ANYTHING IN MY FACE THAT... THAT TELLS YOU?
LOOK, YOU'RE PROBABLY VERY SICK.
YOU'VE GOT DELUSIONS OR SOMETHING.
POP...
I DON'T WANT TO HURT YOU, AND I DON'T WANT TO GET YOU IN TROUBLE.
YOU BETTER GO ON, GET OUT OF HERE OR THERE WILL BE TROUBLE.
WHO YOU TALKING TO, ROBERT?

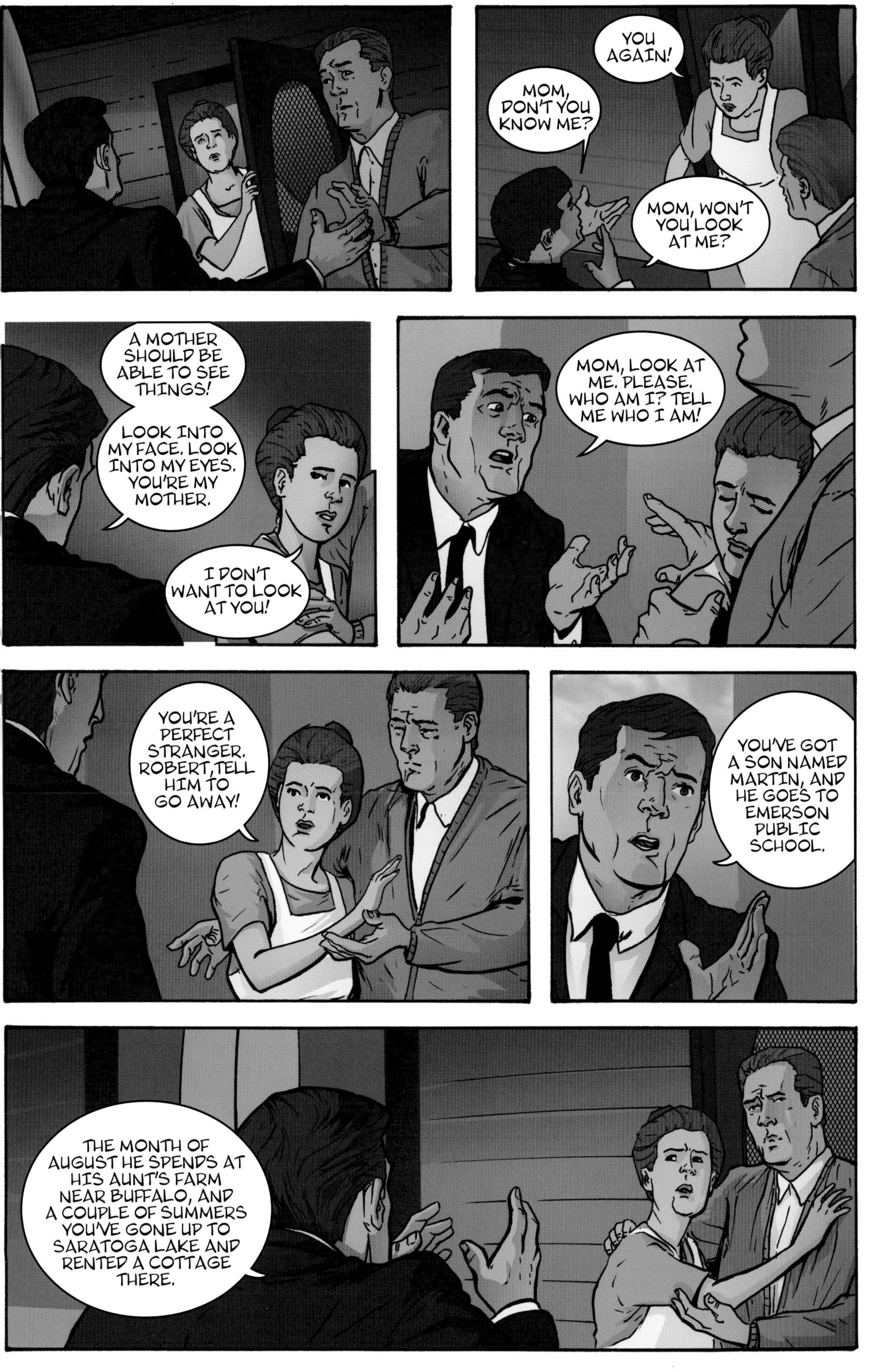
YOU AGAIN!
MOM, DON'T YOU KNOW ME?
MOM, WON'T YOU LOOK AT ME?
A MOTHER SHOULD BE ABLE TO SEE THINGS!
LOOK INTO MY FACE. LOOK INTO MY EYES. YOU'RE MY MOTHER.
I DON'T WANT TO LOOK AT YOU!
MOM, LOOK AT ME. PLEASE. WHO AM I? TELL ME WHO I AM!
YOU'RE A PERFECT STRANGER. ROBERT, TELL HIM TO GO AWAY!
YOU'VE GOT A SON NAMED MARTIN, AND HE GOES TO EMERSON PUBLIC SCHOOL.
THE MONTH OF AUGUST HE SPENDS AT HIS AUNT'S FARM NEAR BUFFALO, AND A COUPLE OF SUMMERS YOU'VE GONE UP TO SARATOGA LAKE AND RENTED A COTTAGE THERE.

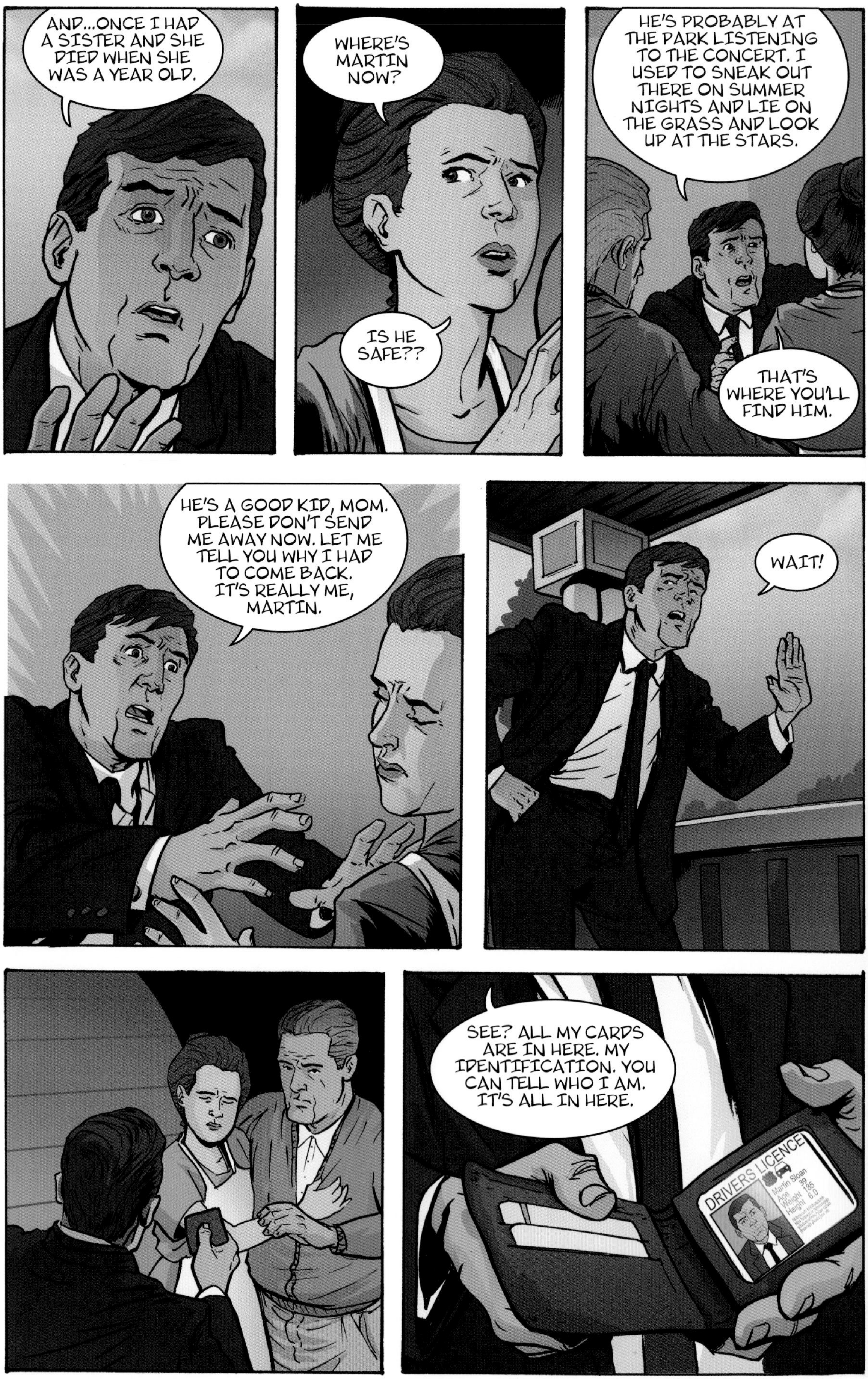
AND...ONCE I HAD A SISTER AND SHE DIED WHEN SHE WAS A YEAR OLD.
WHERE'S MARTIN NOW?
IS HE SAFE??
HE'S PROBABLY AT THE PARK LISTENING TO THE CONCERT. I USED TO SNEAK OUT THERE ON SUMMER NIGHTS AND LIE ON THE GRASS AND LOOK UP AT THE STARS.
THAT'S WHERE YOU'LL FIND HIM.
HE'S A GOOD KID, MOM. PLEASE DON'T SEND ME AWAY NOW. LET ME TELL YOU WHY I HAD TO COME BACK. IT'S REALLY ME, MARTIN.
WAIT!
SEE? ALL MY CARDS ARE IN HERE. MY IDENTIFICATION. YOU CAN TELL WHO I AM. IT'S ALL IN HERE.
DRIVERS LICENCE
Martin Sloan

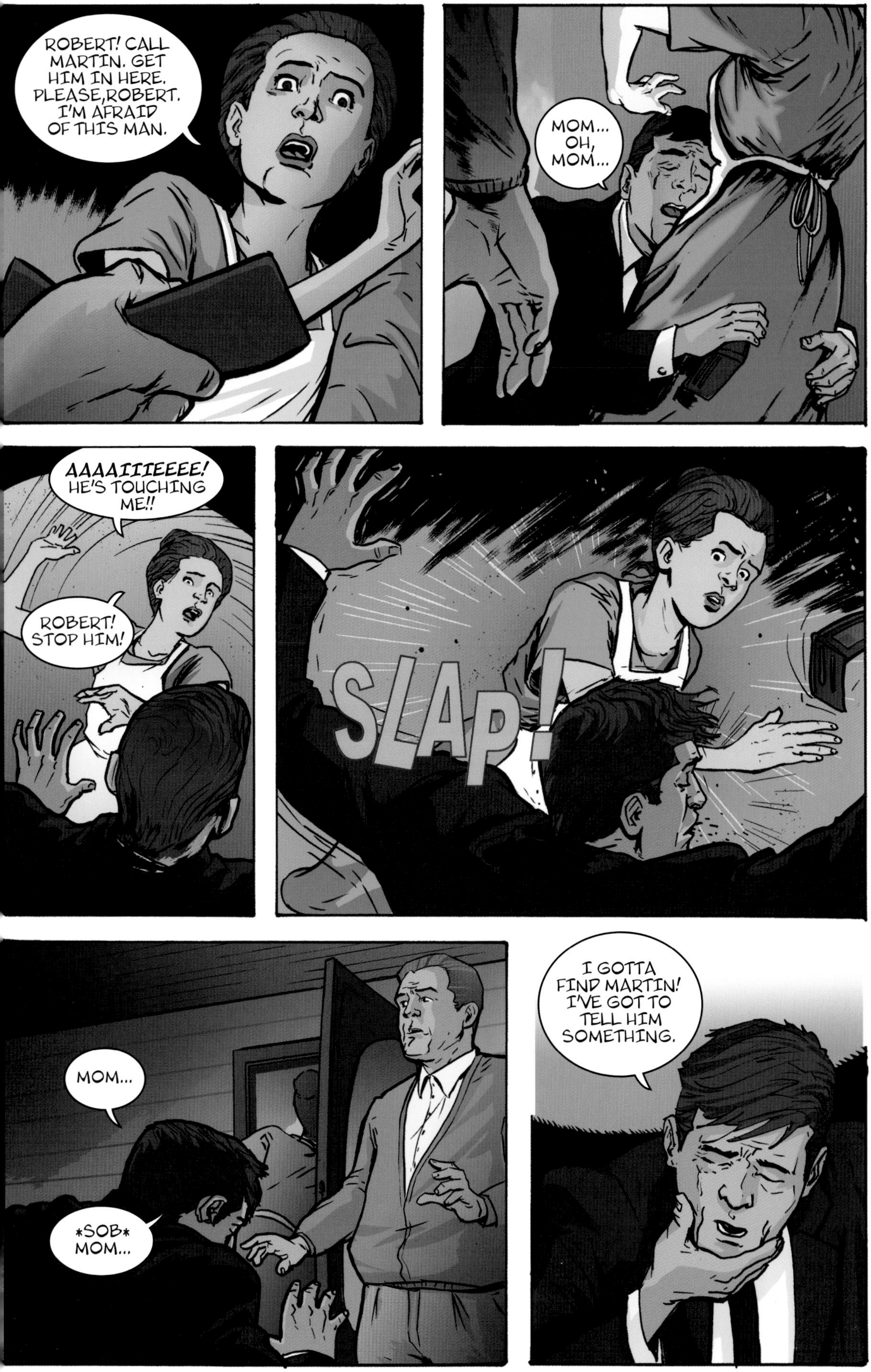
ROBERT! CALL MARTIN. GET HIM IN HERE. PLEASE, ROBERT. I'M AFRAID OF THIS MAN.
MOM... OH, MOM...
AAAAIIIEEEE! HE'S TOUCHING ME!!
ROBERT! STOP HIM!
SLAP!
MOM...
SOB MOM...
I GOTTA FIND MARTIN! I'VE GOT TO TELL HIM SOMETHING.

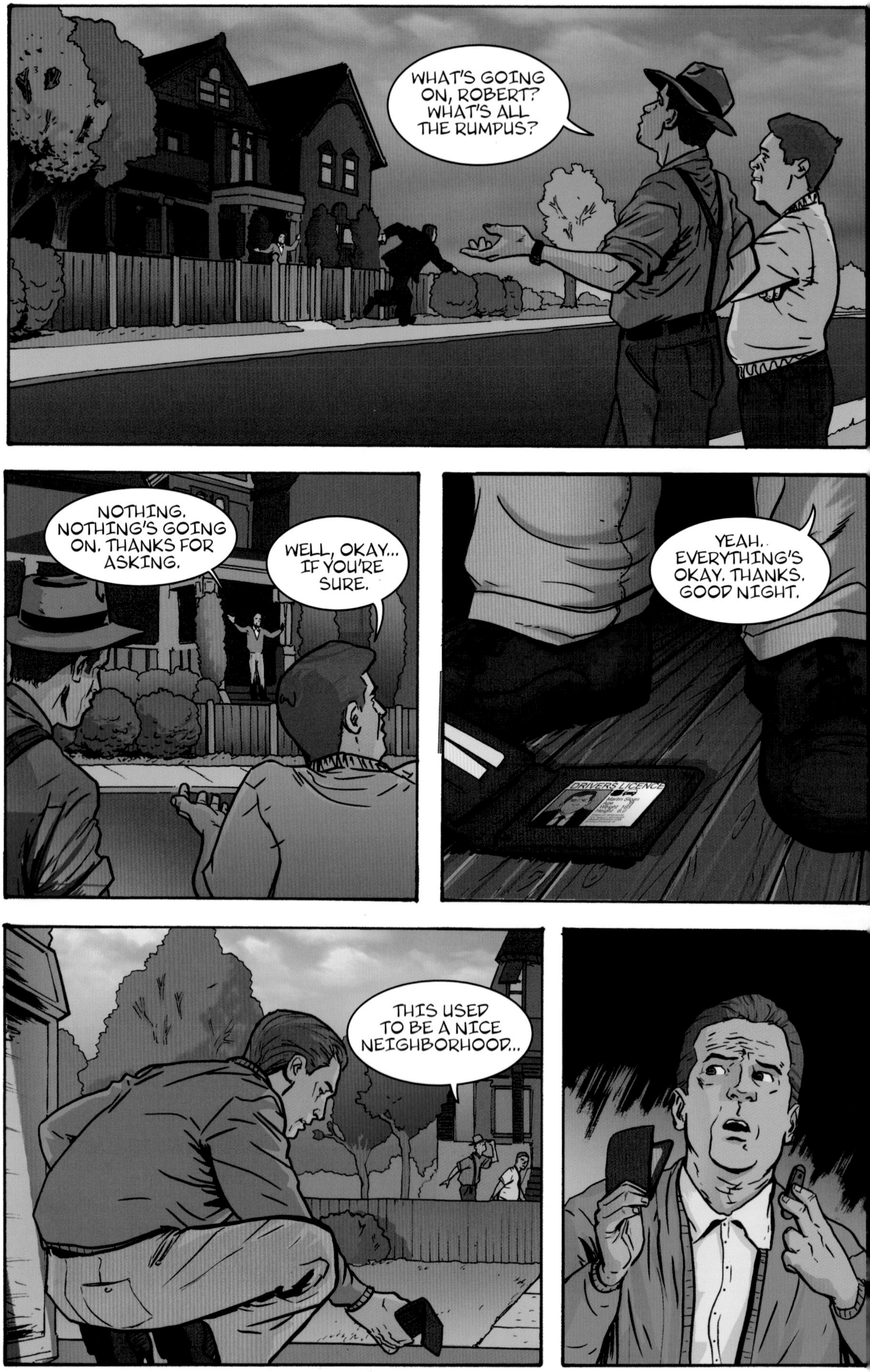
WHAT'S GOING ON, ROBERT? WHAT'S ALL THE RUMPUS?
NOTHING. NOTHING'S GOING ON. THANKS FOR ASKING.
WELL, OKAY... IF YOU'RE SURE.
YEAH. EVERYTHING'S OKAY. THANKS. GOOD NIGHT.
DRIVERS LICENCE
THIS USED TO BE A NICE NEIGHBORHOOD...

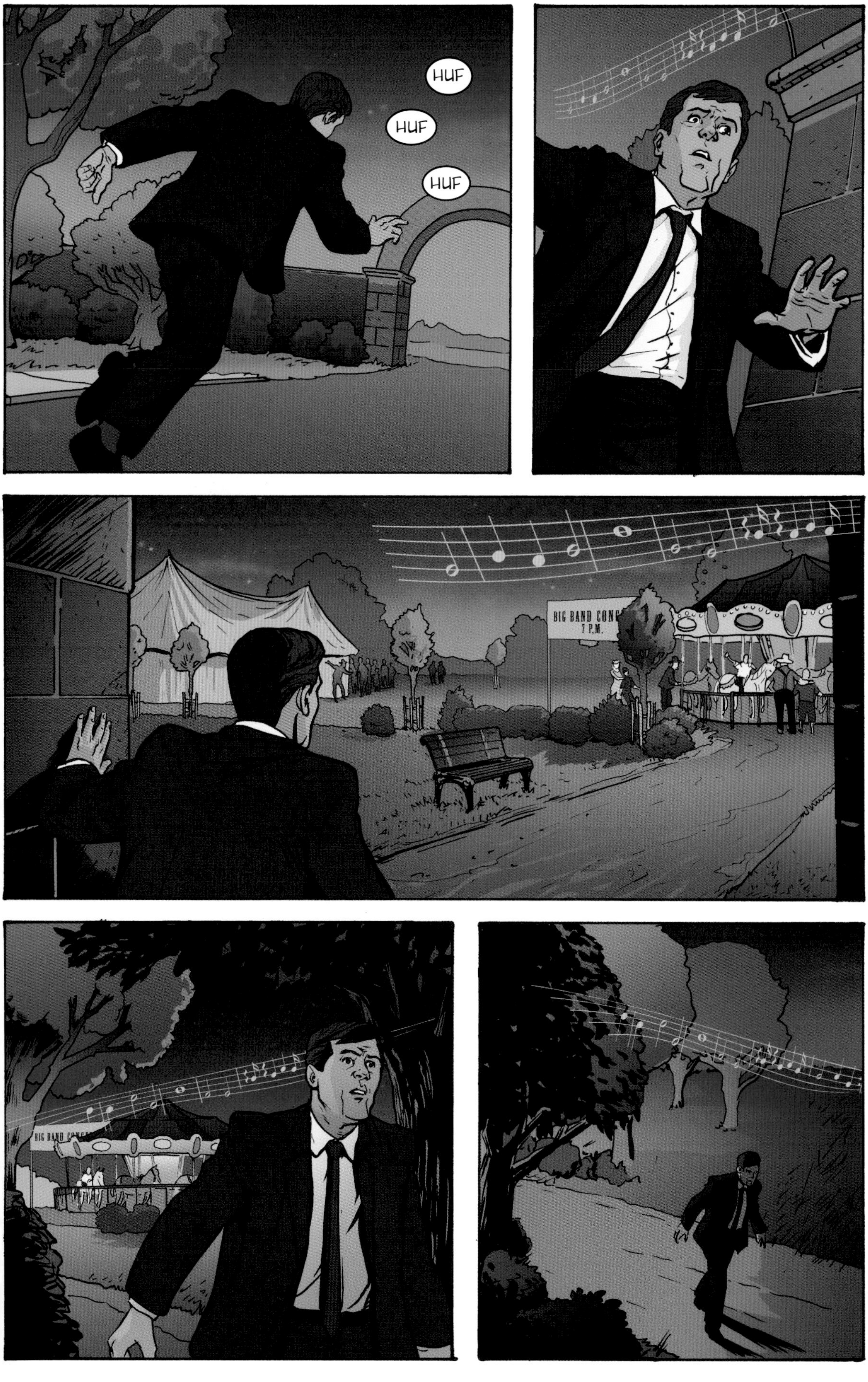
HUF
HUF
HUF
BIG BAND CONC
7 P.M.

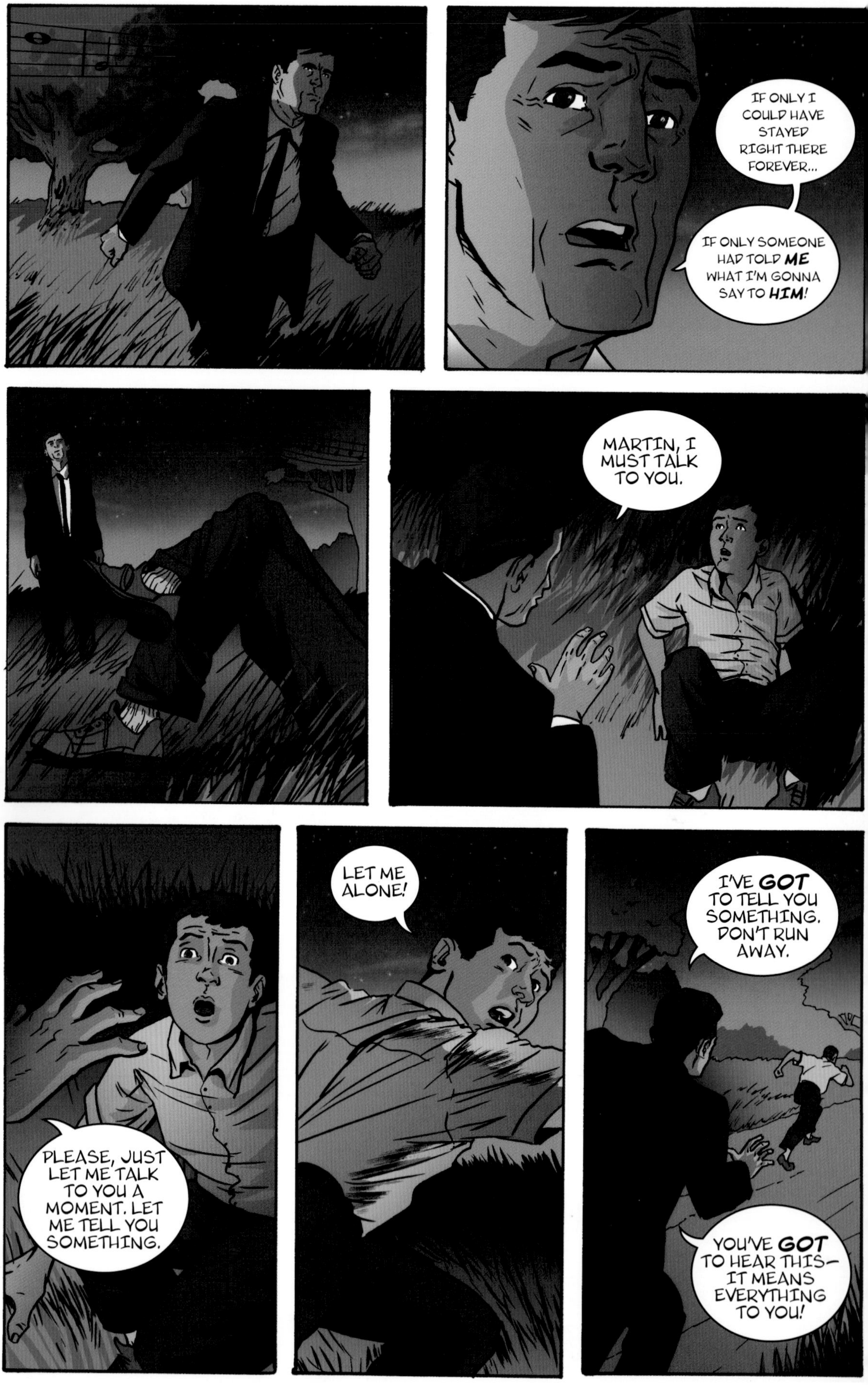
IF ONLY I COULD HAVE STAYED RIGHT THERE FOREVER...
IF ONLY SOMEONE HAD TOLD ME WHAT I'M GONNA SAY TO HIM!
MARTIN, I MUST TALK TO YOU.
PLEASE, JUST LET ME TALK TO YOU A MOMENT. LET ME TELL YOU SOMETHING.
LET ME ALONE!
I'VE GOT TO TELL YOU SOMETHING. DON'T RUN AWAY.
YOU'VE GOT TO HEAR THIS—IT MEANS EVERYTHING TO YOU!

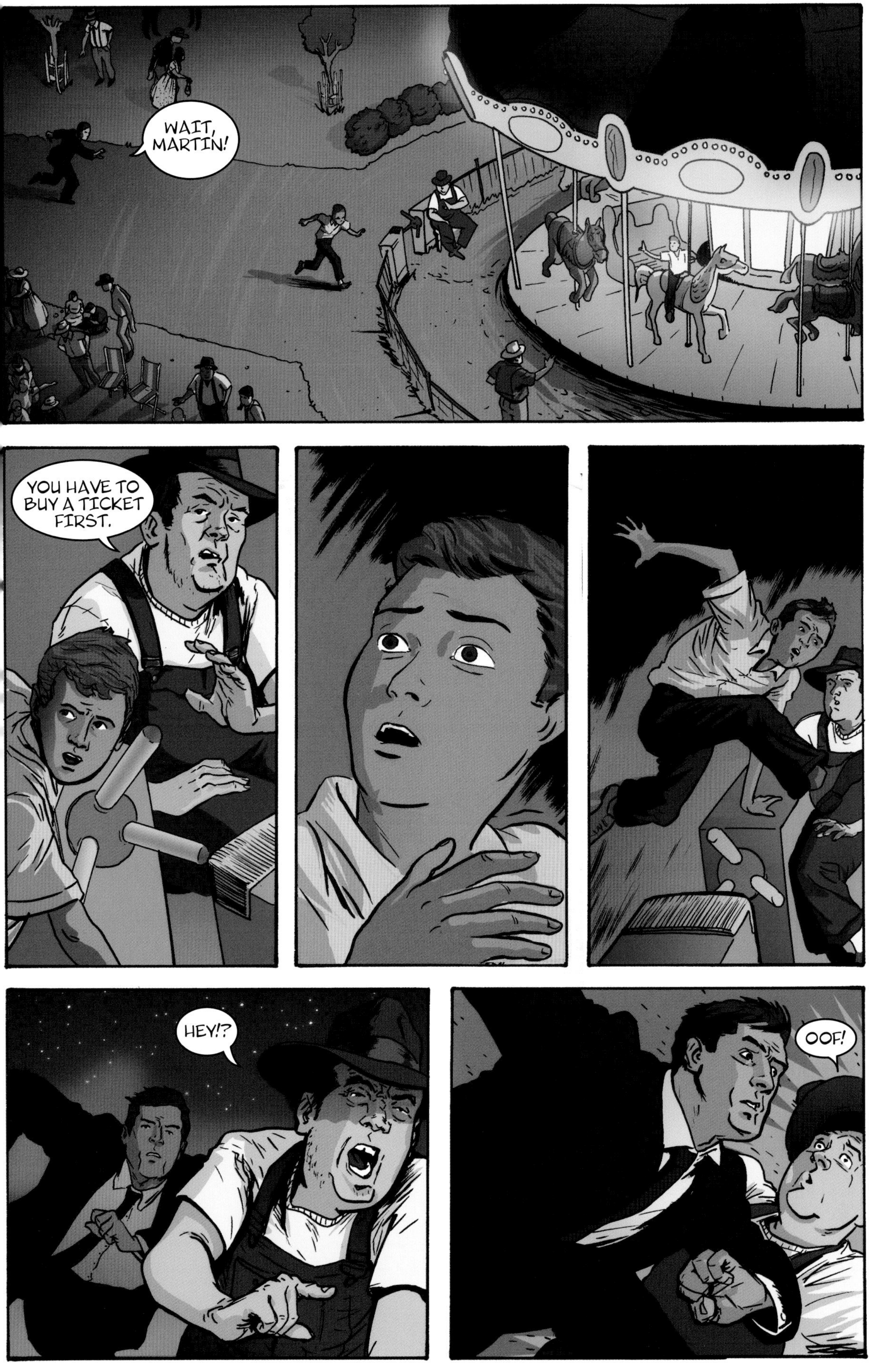
WAIT, MARTIN!
YOU HAVE TO BUY A TICKET FIRST.
HEY!?
OOF!

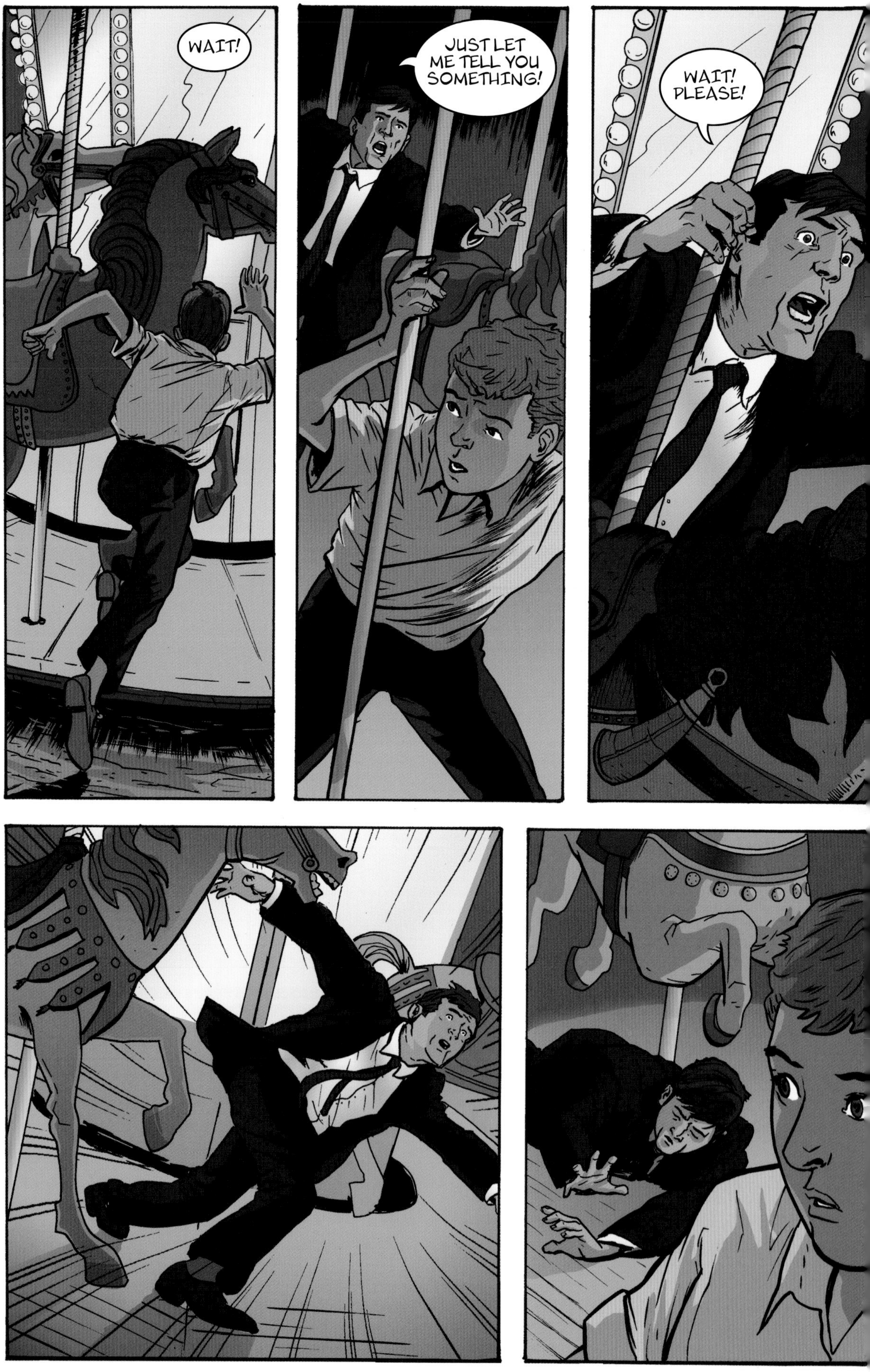
WAIT!
JUST LET ME TELL YOU SOMETHING!
WAIT! PLEASE!

HOLD ON, MISTER. LET ME GIVE YOU A HAND.

I JUST WANT TO TELL YOU SOMETHING. I JUST NEED TO TALK TO YOU FOR ONE MOMENT, JUST ONE.

MARTIN, WATCH OUT!

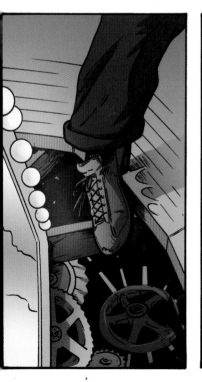

WATCH OUT!

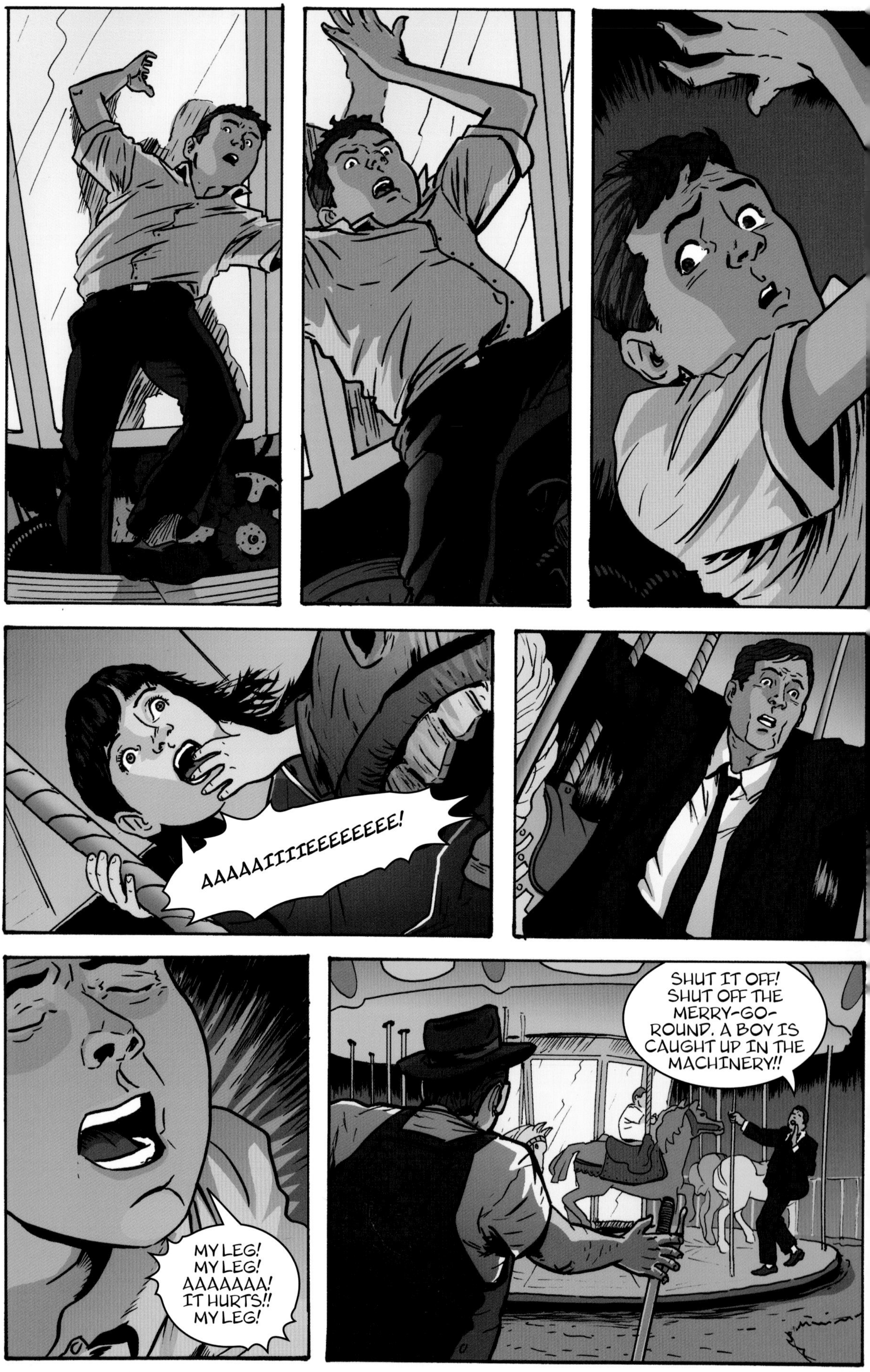
AAAAAIIIIEEEEEEEE!
MY LEG! MY LEG! AAAAAAA! IT HURTS!! MY LEG!
SHUT IT OFF! SHUT OFF THE MERRY-GO-ROUND. A BOY IS CAUGHT UP IN THE MACHINERY!!

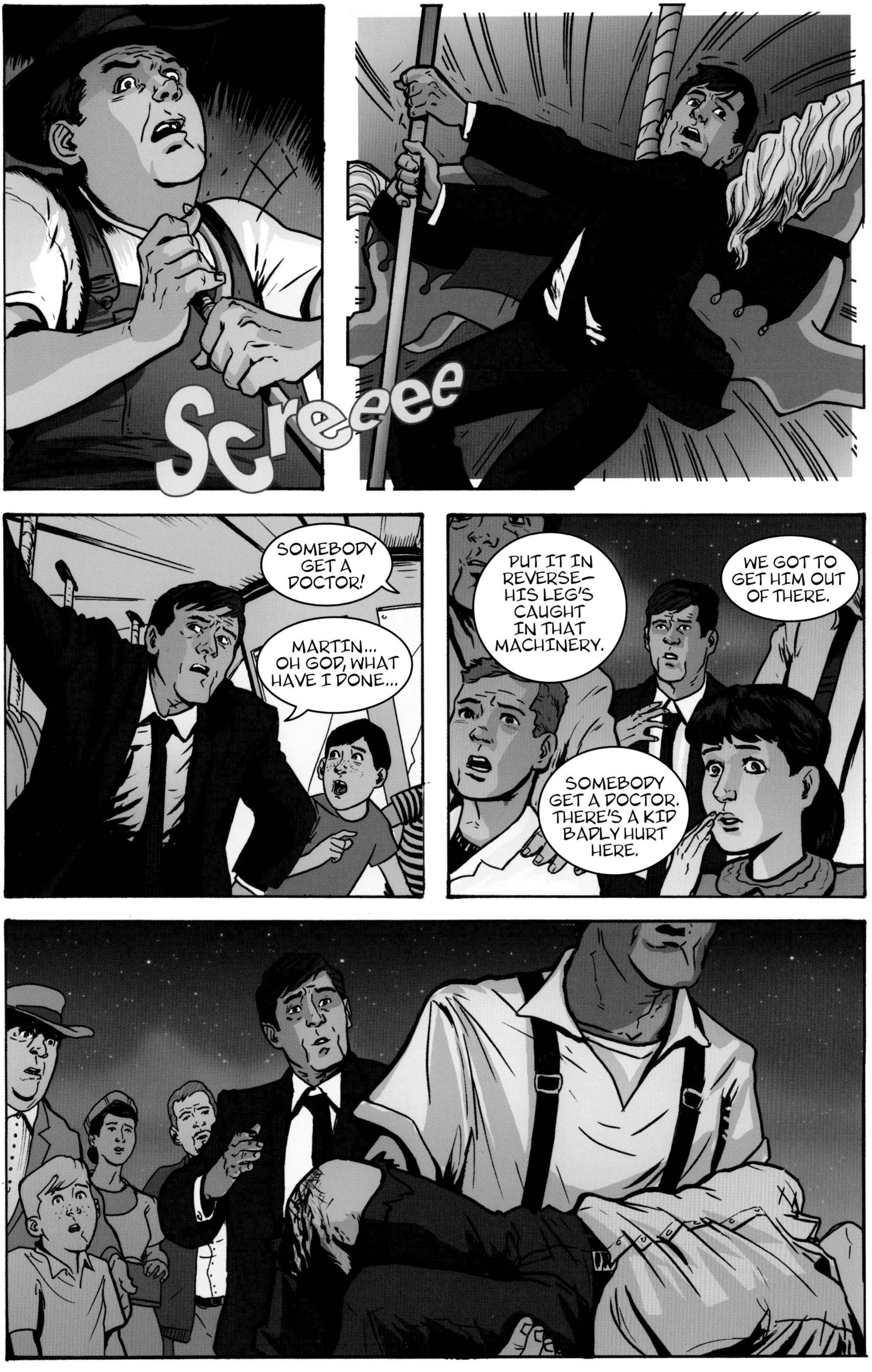
Screeee
SOMEBODY GET A DOCTOR!
MARTIN... OH GOD, WHAT HAVE I DONE...
PUT IT IN REVERSE— HIS LEG'S CAUGHT IN THAT MACHINERY.
WE GOT TO GET HIM OUT OF THERE.
SOMEBODY GET A DOCTOR. THERE'S A KID BADLY HURT HERE.

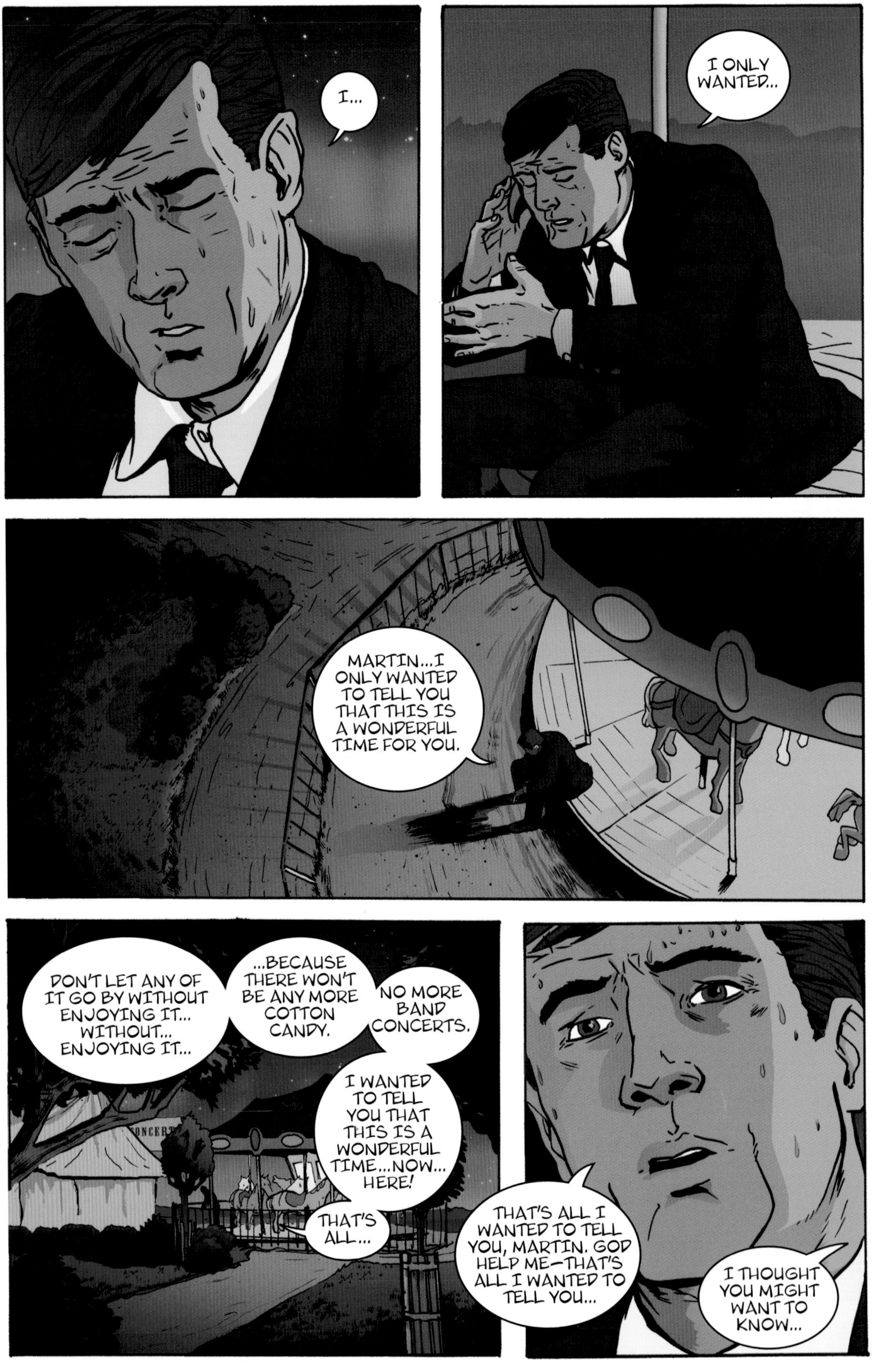
I...
I ONLY WANTED...
MARTIN...I ONLY WANTED TO TELL YOU THAT THIS IS A WONDERFUL TIME FOR YOU.
DON'T LET ANY OF IT GO BY WITHOUT ENJOYING IT... WITHOUT... ENJOYING IT...
...BECAUSE THERE WON'T BE ANY MORE COTTON CANDY.
NO MORE BAND CONCERTS.
I WANTED TO TELL YOU THAT THIS IS A WONDERFUL TIME...NOW... HERE!
THAT'S ALL...
THAT'S ALL I WANTED TO TELL YOU, MARTIN. GOD HELP ME—THAT'S ALL I WANTED TO TELL YOU...
I THOUGHT YOU MIGHT WANT TO KNOW...

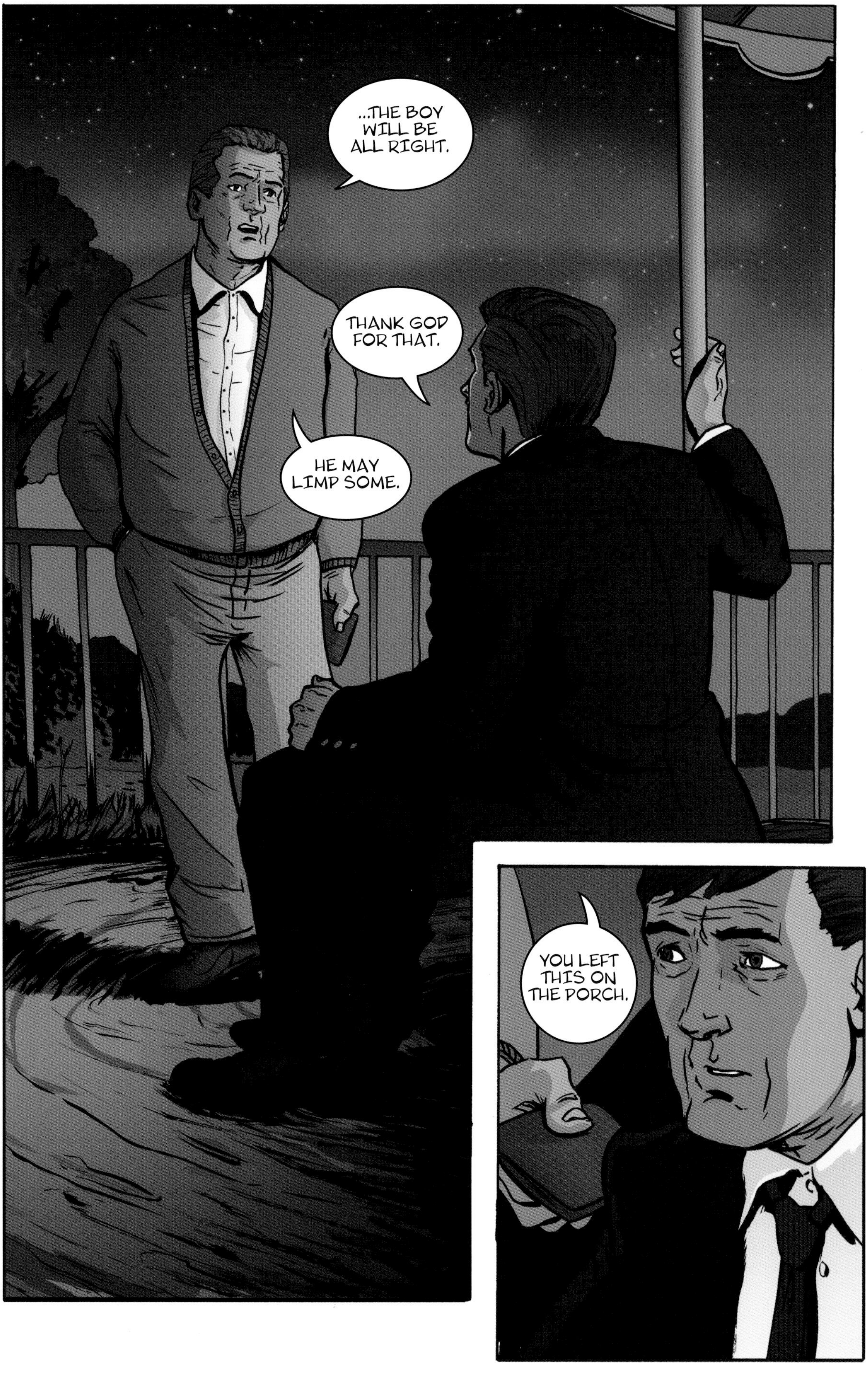
...THE BOY WILL BE ALL RIGHT.
THANK GOD FOR THAT.
HE MAY LIMP SOME.
YOU LEFT THIS ON THE PORCH.

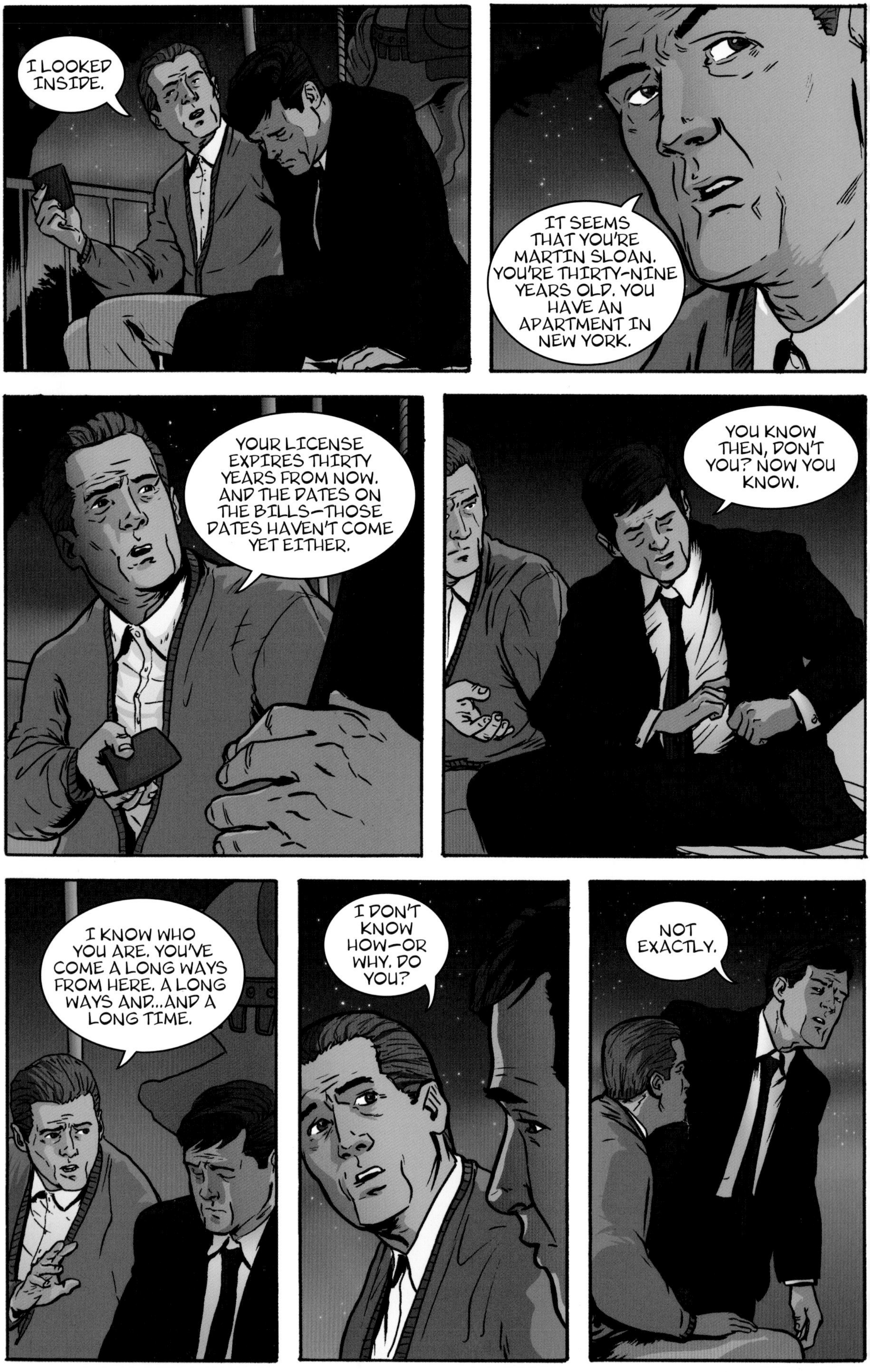
I LOOKED INSIDE.
IT SEEMS THAT YOU'RE MARTIN SLOAN. YOU'RE THIRTY-NINE YEARS OLD. YOU HAVE AN APARTMENT IN NEW YORK.
YOUR LICENSE EXPIRES THIRTY YEARS FROM NOW. AND THE DATES ON THE BILLS—THOSE DATES HAVEN'T COME YET EITHER.
YOU KNOW THEN, DON'T YOU? NOW YOU KNOW.
I KNOW WHO YOU ARE. YOU'VE COME A LONG WAYS FROM HERE. A LONG WAYS AND...AND A LONG TIME.
I DON'T KNOW HOW—OR WHY. DO YOU?
NOT EXACTLY.

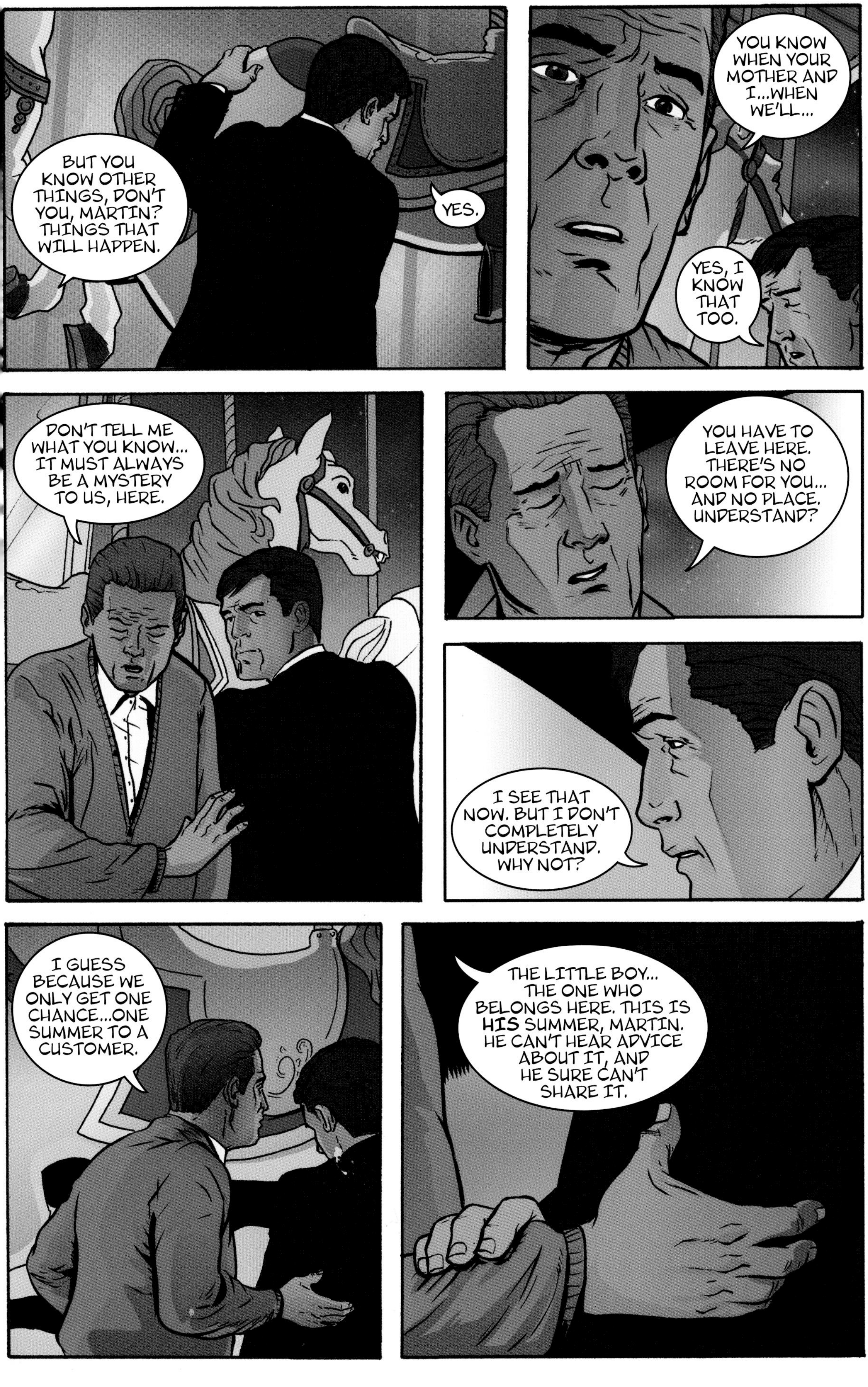
BUT YOU KNOW OTHER THINGS, DON'T YOU, MARTIN? THINGS THAT WILL HAPPEN.
YES.
YOU KNOW WHEN YOUR MOTHER AND I...WHEN WE'LL...
YES, I KNOW THAT TOO.
DON'T TELL ME WHAT YOU KNOW... IT MUST ALWAYS BE A MYSTERY TO US, HERE.
YOU HAVE TO LEAVE HERE. THERE'S NO ROOM FOR YOU... AND NO PLACE. UNDERSTAND?
I SEE THAT NOW. BUT I DON'T COMPLETELY UNDERSTAND. WHY NOT?
I GUESS BECAUSE WE ONLY GET ONE CHANCE...ONE SUMMER TO A CUSTOMER.
THE LITTLE BOY... THE ONE WHO BELONGS HERE. THIS IS **HIS** SUMMER, MARTIN. HE CAN'T HEAR ADVICE ABOUT IT, AND HE SURE CAN'T SHARE IT.

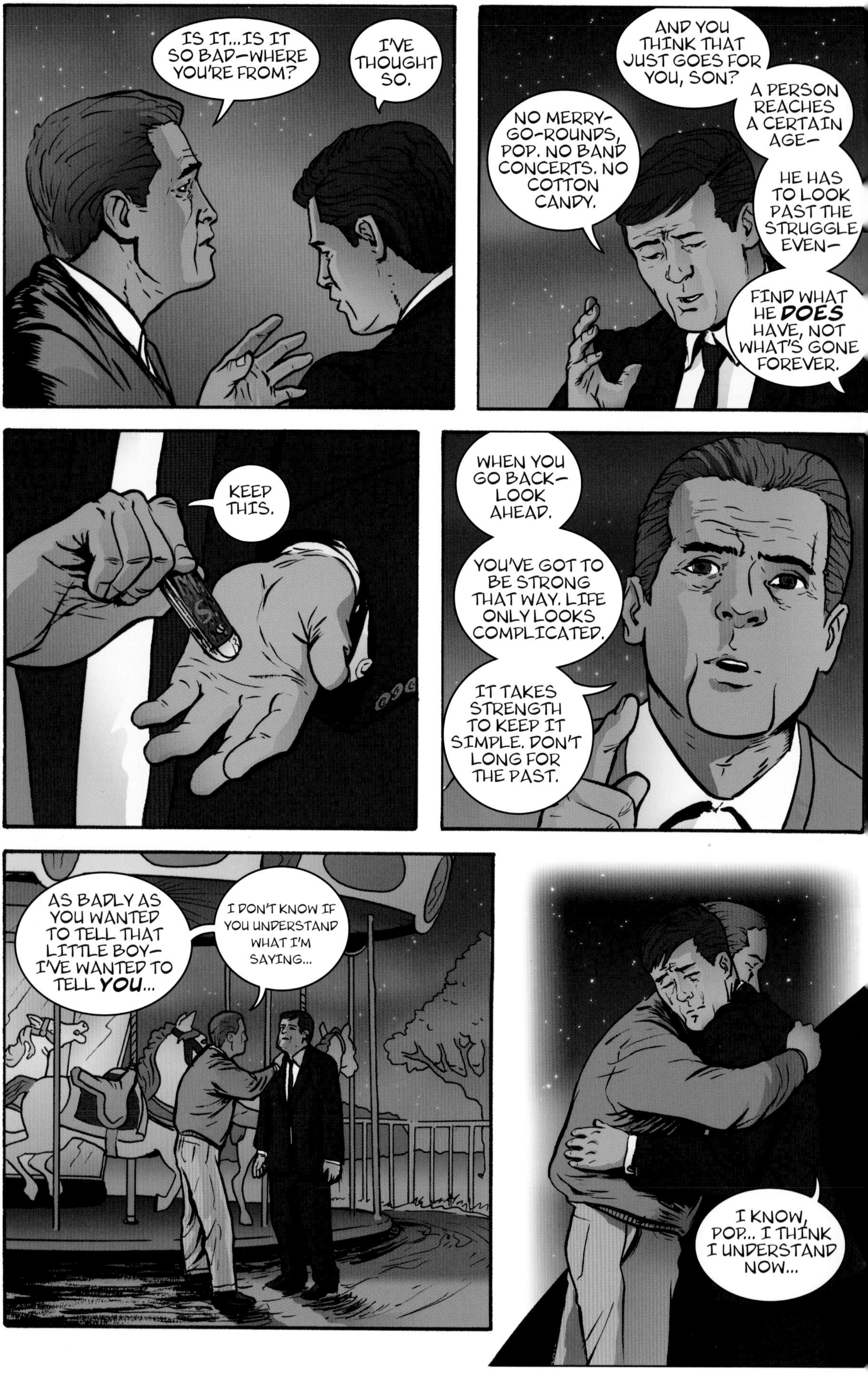
IS IT... IS IT SO BAD—WHERE YOU'RE FROM?
I'VE THOUGHT SO.
NO MERRY-GO-ROUNDS, POP. NO BAND CONCERTS. NO COTTON CANDY.
AND YOU THINK THAT JUST GOES FOR YOU, SON?
A PERSON REACHES A CERTAIN AGE—
HE HAS TO LOOK PAST THE STRUGGLE EVEN—
FIND WHAT HE **DOES** HAVE, NOT WHAT'S GONE FOREVER.
KEEP THIS.
WHEN YOU GO BACK—LOOK AHEAD.
YOU'VE GOT TO BE STRONG THAT WAY. LIFE ONLY LOOKS COMPLICATED.
IT TAKES STRENGTH TO KEEP IT SIMPLE. DON'T LONG FOR THE PAST.
AS BADLY AS YOU WANTED TO TELL THAT LITTLE BOY—I'VE WANTED TO TELL **YOU**...
I DON'T KNOW IF YOU UNDERSTAND WHAT I'M SAYING...
I KNOW, POP... I THINK I UNDERSTAND NOW...

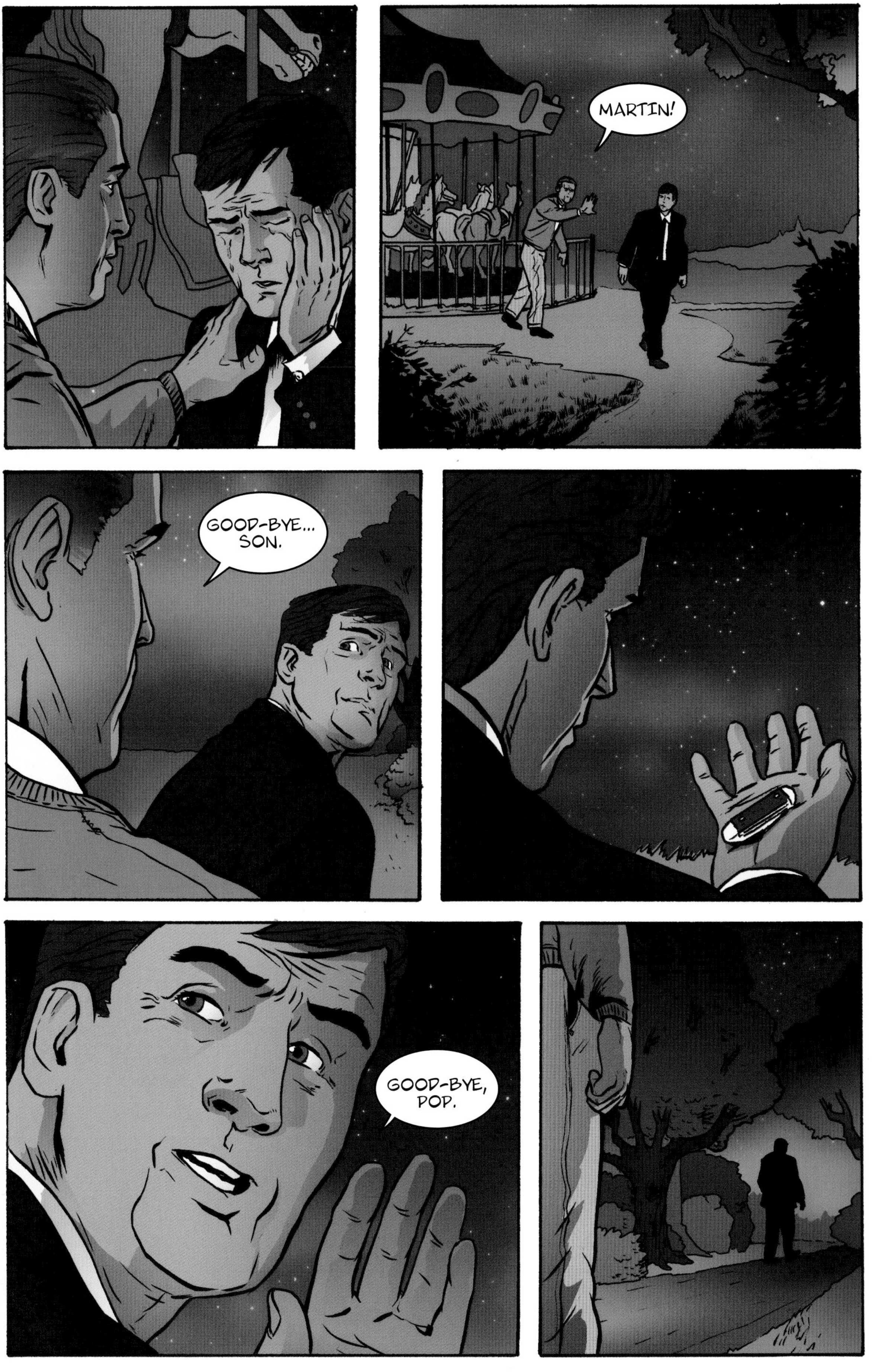
MARTIN!
GOOD-BYE... SON.
GOOD-BYE, POP.

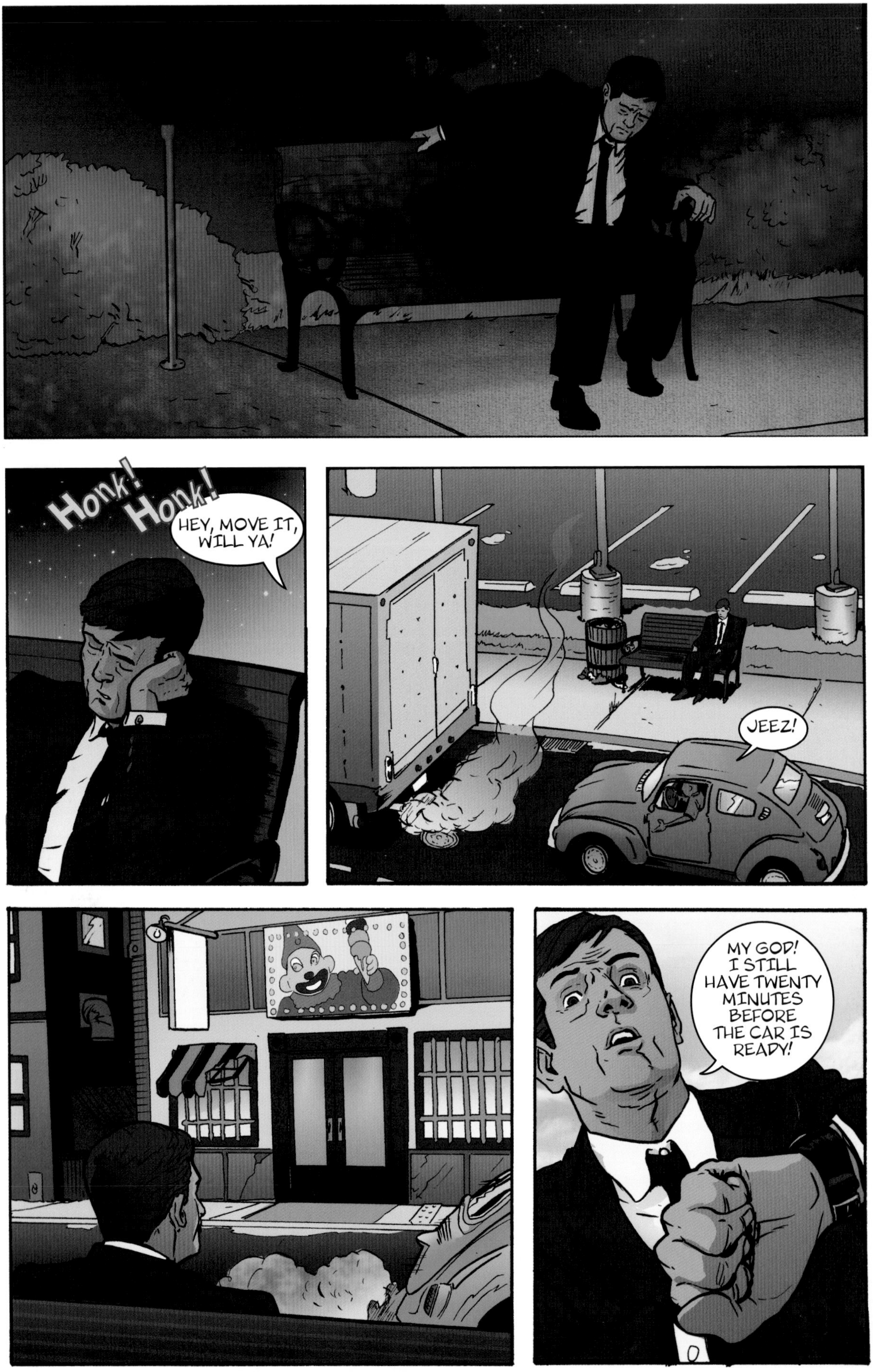
Honk! Honk!
HEY, MOVE IT, WILL YA!
JEEZ!
MY GOD! I STILL HAVE TWENTY MINUTES BEFORE THE CAR IS READY!

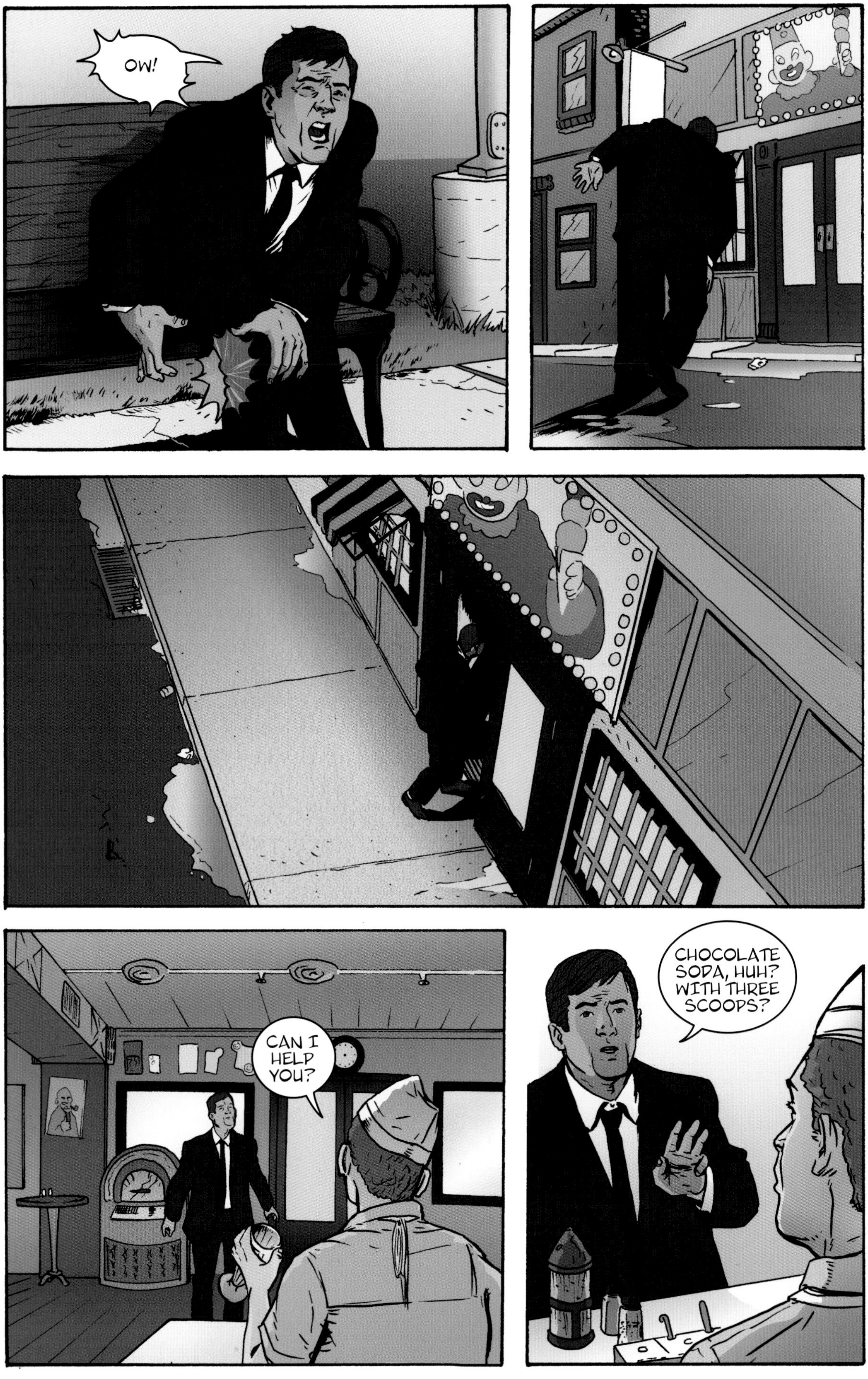
OW!
CAN I HELP YOU?
CHOCOLATE SODA, HUH? WITH THREE SCOOPS?

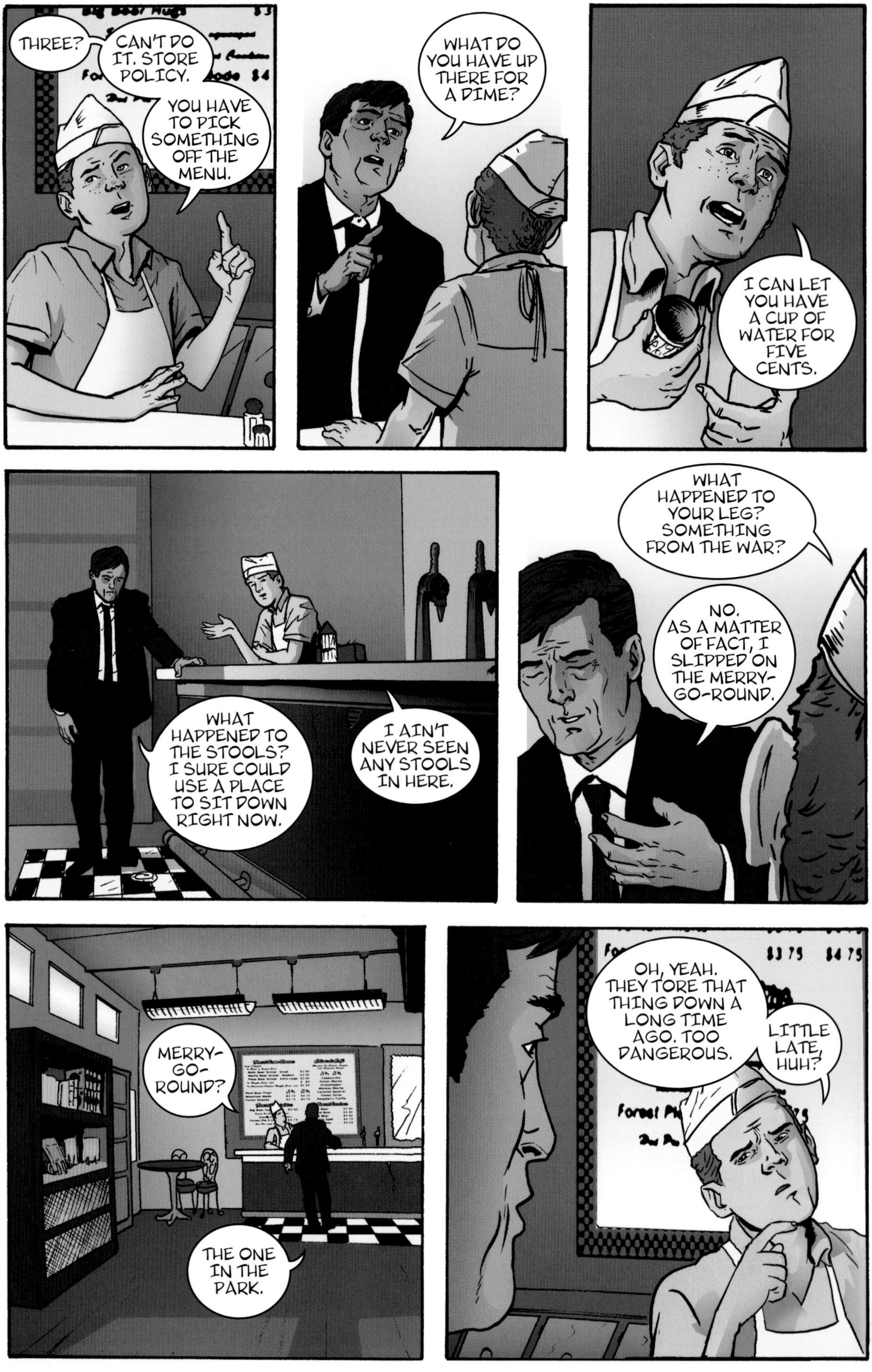
THREE?
CAN'T DO IT. STORE POLICY.
YOU HAVE TO PICK SOMETHING OFF THE MENU.
WHAT DO YOU HAVE UP THERE FOR A DIME?
I CAN LET YOU HAVE A CUP OF WATER FOR FIVE CENTS.
WHAT HAPPENED TO THE STOOLS? I SURE COULD USE A PLACE TO SIT DOWN RIGHT NOW.
I AIN'T NEVER SEEN ANY STOOLS IN HERE.
WHAT HAPPENED TO YOUR LEG? SOMETHING FROM THE WAR?
NO. AS A MATTER OF FACT, I SLIPPED ON THE MERRY-GO-ROUND.
MERRY-GO-ROUND?
THE ONE IN THE PARK.
OH, YEAH. THEY TORE THAT THING DOWN A LONG TIME AGO. TOO DANGEROUS.
LITTLE LATE, HUH?

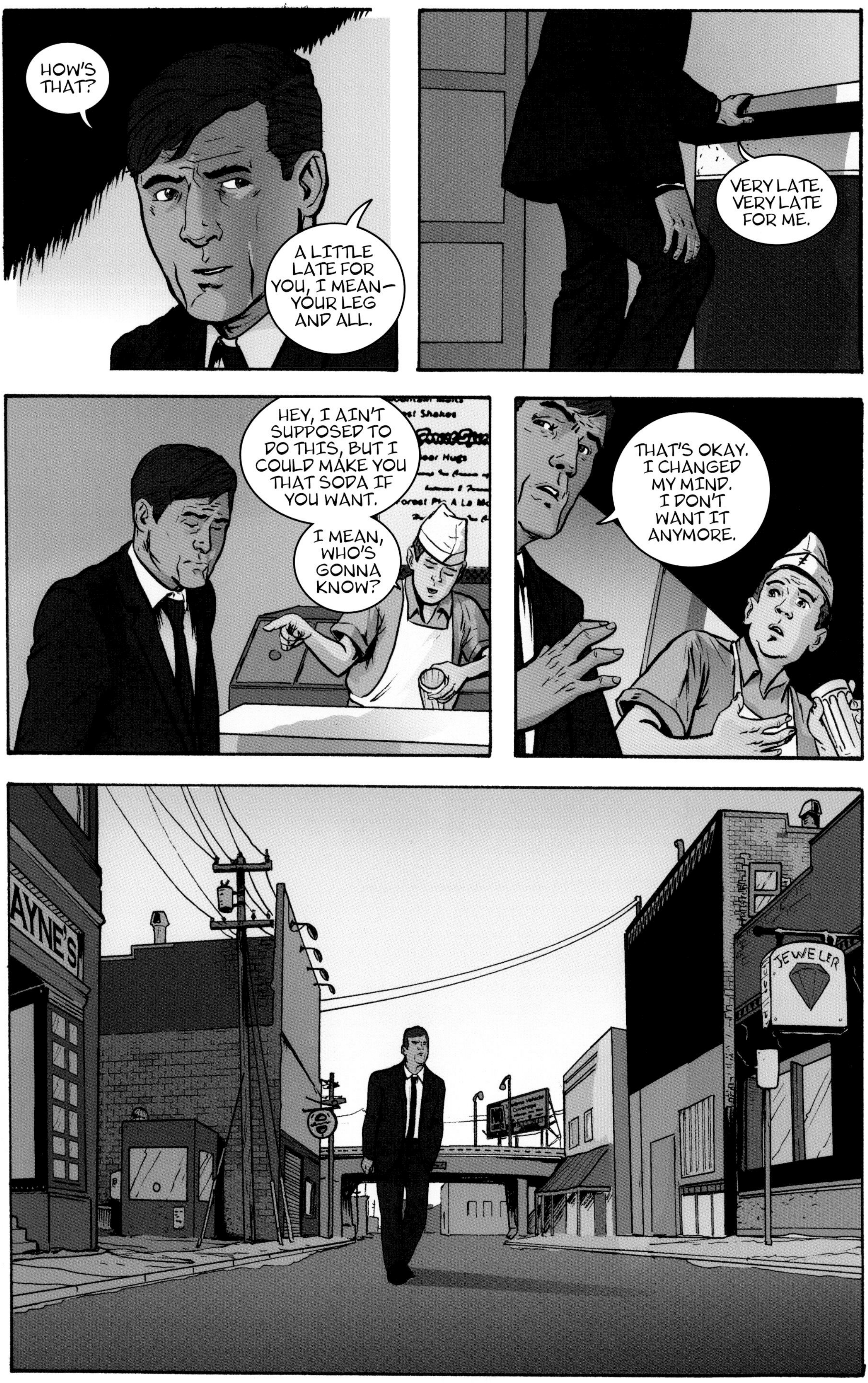
HOW'S THAT?
A LITTLE LATE FOR YOU, I MEAN—YOUR LEG AND ALL.
VERY LATE. VERY LATE FOR ME.
HEY, I AIN'T SUPPOSED TO DO THIS, BUT I COULD MAKE YOU THAT SODA IF YOU WANT.
I MEAN, WHO'S GONNA KNOW?
THAT'S OKAY. I CHANGED MY MIND. I DON'T WANT IT ANYMORE.
AYNE'S
JEWELER

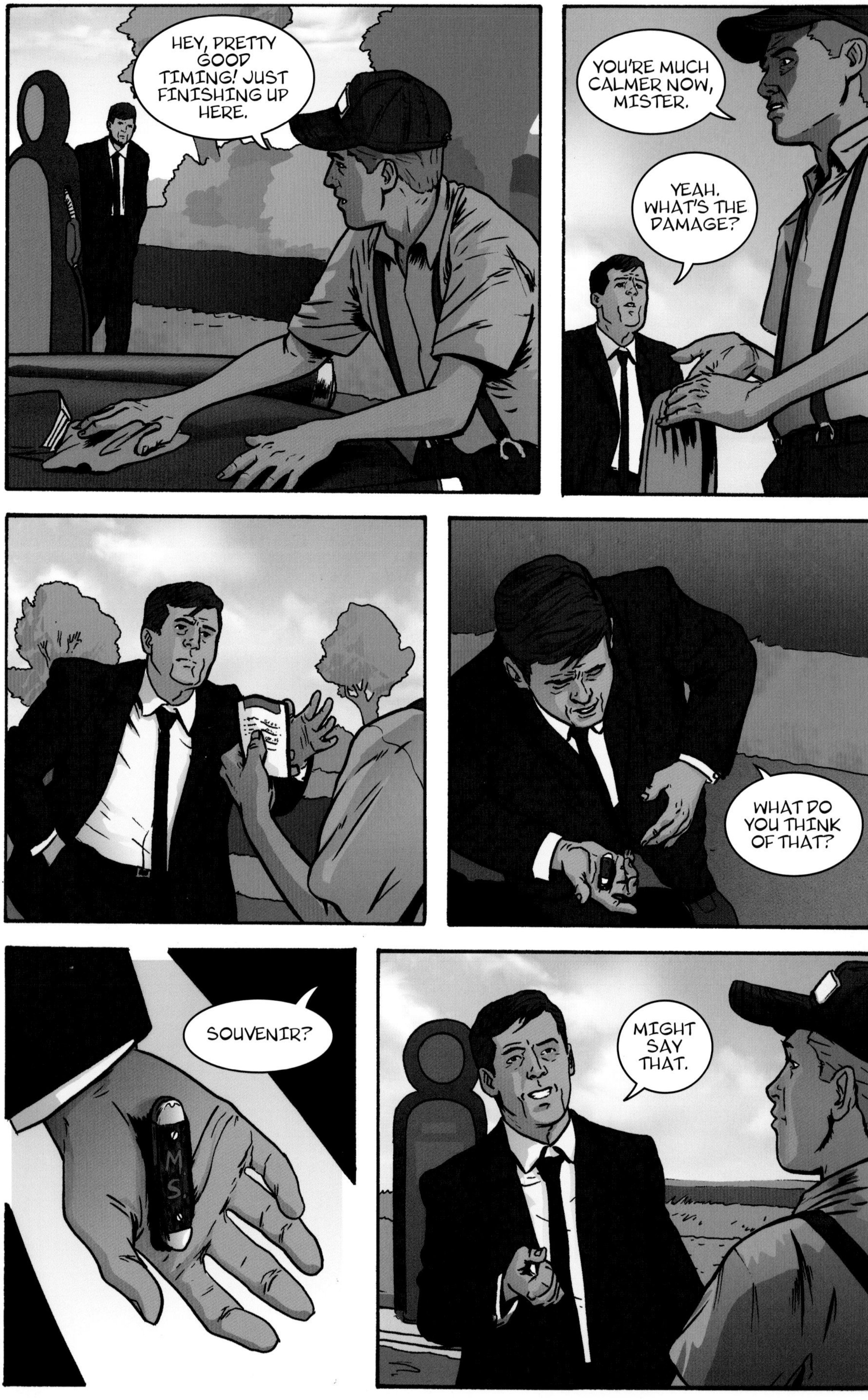
HEY, PRETTY GOOD TIMING! JUST FINISHING UP HERE.
YOU'RE MUCH CALMER NOW, MISTER.
YEAH. WHAT'S THE DAMAGE?
WHAT DO YOU THINK OF THAT?
SOUVENIR?
M.S.
MIGHT SAY THAT.

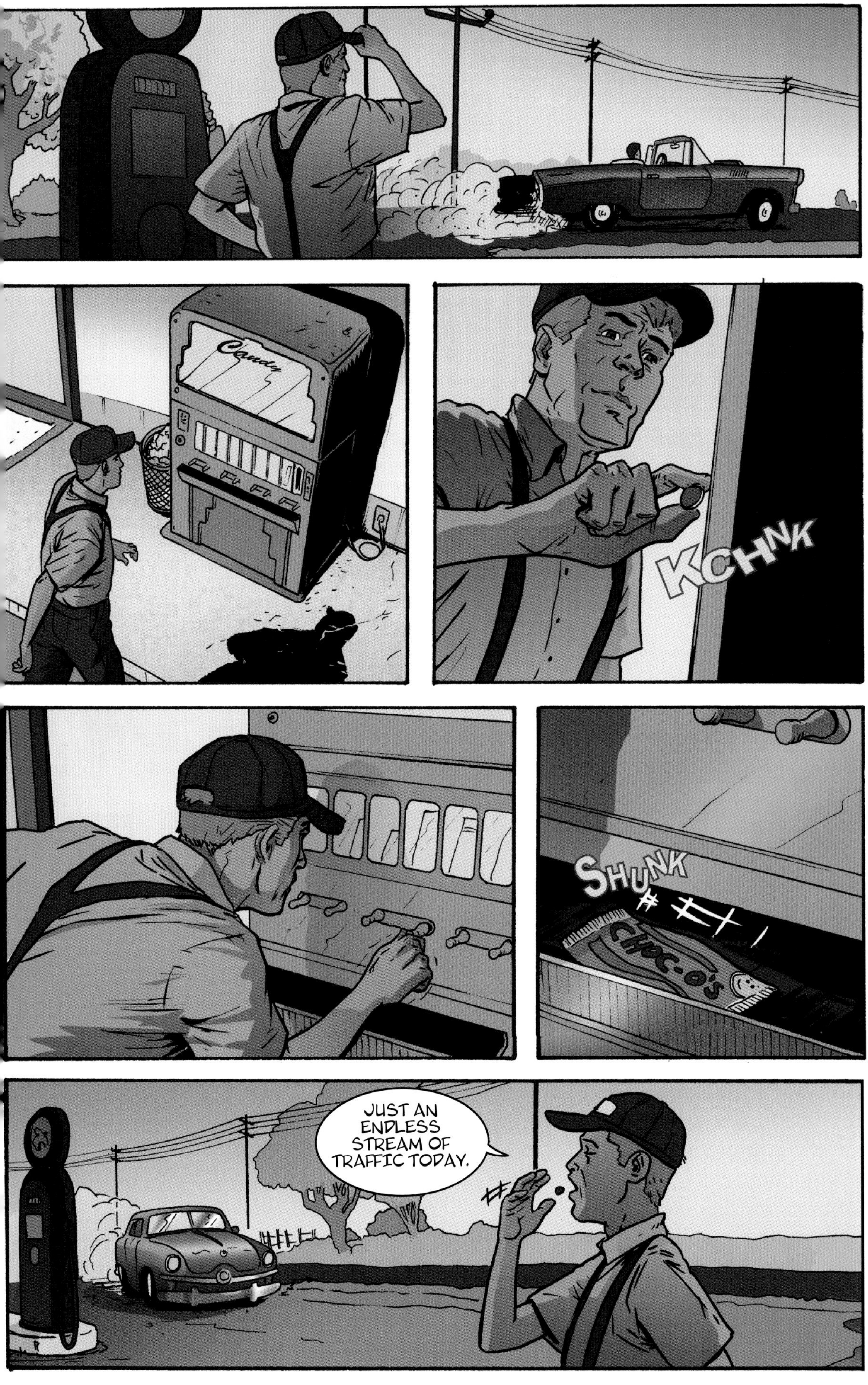
Candy
KCHNK
SHUNK
CHOC-O'S
JUST AN ENDLESS STREAM OF TRAFFIC TODAY.

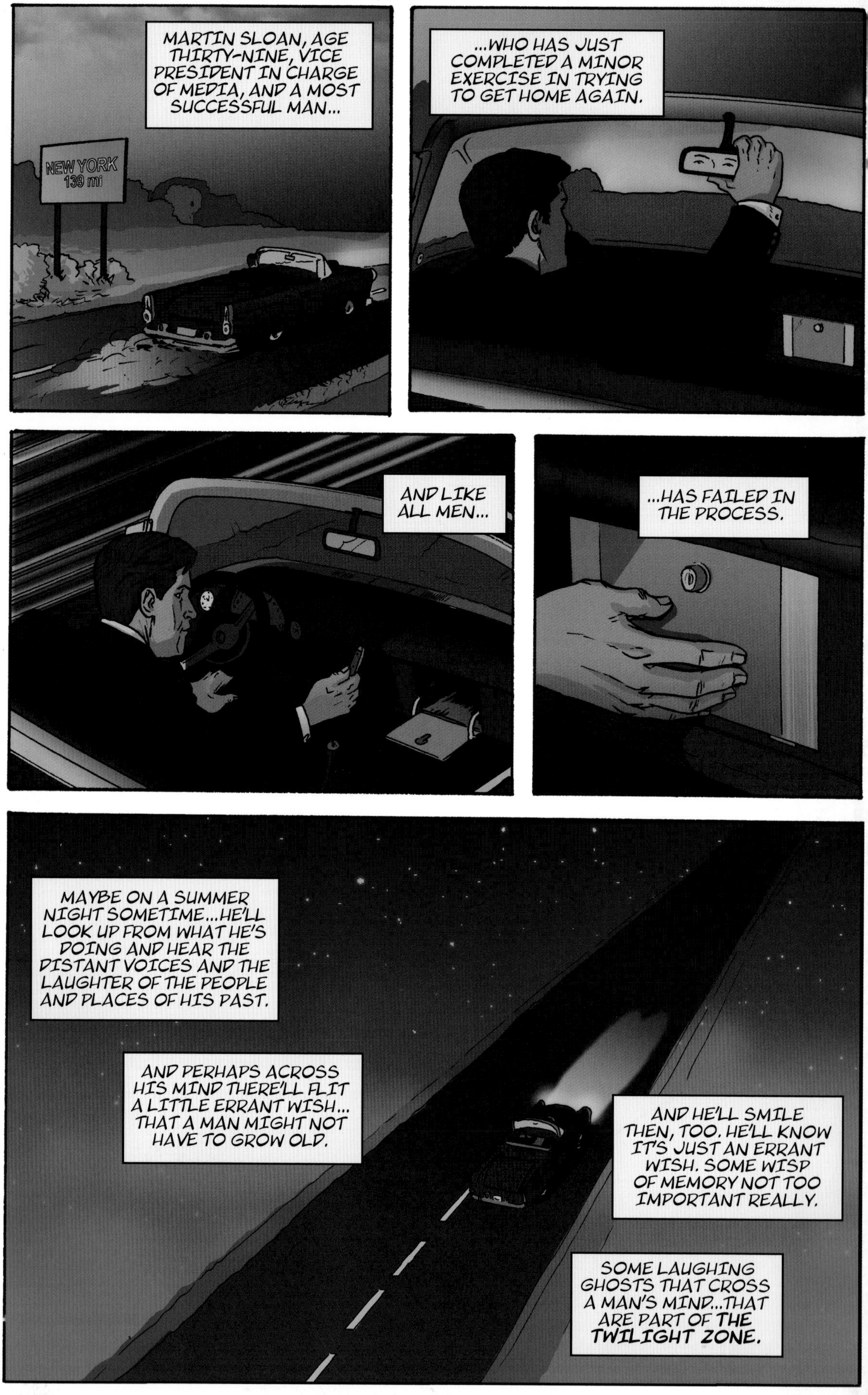
MARTIN SLOAN, AGE THIRTY-NINE, VICE PRESIDENT IN CHARGE OF MEDIA, AND A MOST SUCCESSFUL MAN...
NEW YORK 139 mi
...WHO HAS JUST COMPLETED A MINOR EXERCISE IN TRYING TO GET HOME AGAIN.
AND LIKE ALL MEN...
...HAS FAILED IN THE PROCESS.
MAYBE ON A SUMMER NIGHT SOMETIME...HE'LL LOOK UP FROM WHAT HE'S DOING AND HEAR THE DISTANT VOICES AND THE LAUGHTER OF THE PEOPLE AND PLACES OF HIS PAST.
AND PERHAPS ACROSS HIS MIND THERE'LL FLIT A LITTLE ERRANT WISH... THAT A MAN MIGHT NOT HAVE TO GROW OLD.
AND HE'LL SMILE THEN, TOO. HE'LL KNOW IT'S JUST AN ERRANT WISH. SOME WISP OF MEMORY NOT TOO IMPORTANT REALLY.
SOME LAUGHING GHOSTS THAT CROSS A MAN'S MIND...THAT ARE PART OF THE TWILIGHT ZONE.

Walking Distance

Season One, Episode #5

Original Air Date: October 30, 1959

Written by Rod Serling

Cast

Narrator: Rod Serling

Martin Sloan: Gig Young

Robert Sloan (Martin's Father): Frank Overton *
*Also appeared in *Mute* as Harry Wheeler

Martin's Mother: Irene Tedrow *
*Also appeared in *The Lateness of the Hour* as Mrs. Loren

Martin as a Boy: Michael Montgomery

The Wilcox Boy: Ron Howard

Charlie: Byron Foulger

Gas Station Attendant: Sheridan Comerate

Soda Jerk: Joseph Corey

Teenager: Buzz Martin

Woman in Park: Nan Peterson *
*Also appeared in *The Whole Truth* as Young Woman and *From Agnes—With Love* as the Secretary

Mr. Wilson: Pat O'Malley *
*Also appeared in *Back There* as an Attendant and *Static* as Mr. Llewellyn

Crew

Producer: Buck Houghton

Director: Robert Stevens

Director of Photography: George T. Clemens

Music: Bernard Herrmann

Film Editor: Joseph Gluck

Production Note

Walking Distance is considered to be Serling's most personal episode. It's based on his memories of growing up in Binghamton, New York, and is said to be inspired by that city's Recreation Park—which has a carousel, a bandstand, and a plaque commemorating this episode.

ADAPTING STORIES FROM ROD SERLING'S
THE TWILIGHT ZONE

In terms of screenwriting adaptations it's trying to cut out stuff that's extraneous, without doing damage to the original piece, because you owe a debt of some respect to the original author.

—Rod Serling, 1975

At first, the idea sounded straightforward. Take an original *Twilight Zone* screenplay and adapt it into a graphic novel—break the visuals into panels, move the dialogue into balloons and captions. After all, Rod Serling himself was a fan of comics, and graphic novels are their visual and literary heirs. Serling collected Entertaining Comics titles such as *Tales from the Crypt* and *Weird Science*, the themes of which resonate in *The Twilight Zone*; even Serling's trademark narration could be considered an echo of the Crypt Keeper's introductions. Yet the more I considered the task of adapting the scripts, the more the gravity of what I was doing set in. I grew up watching *The Twilight Zone*, after all, as did so many Americans. The work required a certain reverential perspective, considering the show's iconic status, not to mention the quality of the original material.

In the 1950s the comics Serling had enjoyed were considered subversive, a threat to America's youth. Frederick Wertham published *Seduction of the Innocent* in 1954, excoriating comics in an atmosphere of public paranoia similar to a scene from *The Monsters Are Due on Maple Street*. A year later, a Senate committee was convened to investigate the pernicious influence of horror comics on America's youth, and the Comics Code Authority was established to censor comics' content. EC Comics went out of business as a direct result. In an interesting twist of fate, by the end of the decade *The Twilight Zone* was just beginning to find its television audience with stories that probably would not have made it past the comics censors. Recreating Serling's stories now, in graphic novel form, seems appropriate, emblematic of an era in which comics are finding a new readership, achieving new respect, and speaking to a new audience receptive to a more sophisticated message.

Serling's stories run the gamut from serious drama, filled with fantastic and frightening dilemmas of the human condition, to wry, tongue-in-cheek humor in a sci-fi wrapper. Selecting eight as graphic novel material meant making difficult choices. Serling was a prolific writer, creating more than half of *The Twilight Zone*'s 156 scripts. It was not only a question of which of these would work best in novelized format, but which ones, as a group, would come closest to capturing the essence of *The Twilight Zone*. The stories ultimately chosen for these books possess the strongest visual possibilities and reflect an effort to achieve a cross section of Serling's dramatic range.

As I began adapting the stories for artists, I immersed myself in the screenplays and watched each episode until I felt I had internalized not just the characters, the plot, and the point, but what I imagined to be something of the author himself. In the process, I felt a growing kinship with Serling. Parts of the screenplay were often deleted from the actual show. Lines, characters, even entire scenes were struck, sometimes for budgetary reasons, sometimes because of time constraints, sometimes perhaps because Serling himself may have anticipated problems with the scenes. The show usually had only a thirty-minute time slot. The deleted scenes, however, often add richness and complexity to the story, offering a glimmer into what Serling might have done were it not for the constraints of the television medium. Restoring scenes seemed to help push the story even harder. I felt as if I were developing Serling's original design, following the telling to its logical conclusion.

With each of these stories, I have aspired to take advantage of what the graphic novel format can do. Art and text draw the reader deeply into the narrative. The reader does not just hear, but ponders, actively bridging the gaps between the panels of art with his or her own imagination. The story doesn't just happen to the reader, but, in part, *is* the reader. In other words, *The Twilight Zone* episodes had to be recreated not just to fit into a graphic novel format but to belong to it.

As much as possible, I have endeavored to keep the intentions of the original story intact—that is the "debt of respect" owed to Serling—fully functional in a new medium. From some nearby fifth dimension, I hope Serling is smiling at the prospect of these books, pleased at the thought of a new generation arriving by way of a different avenue perhaps, but entering and being welcomed into the fold of "Zonies" around the world.

—Mark Kneece
Professor of Sequential Art, Savannah College of Art and Design

Acknowledgments

Our thanks go to Carol Serling for her time and consideration while reviewing the adaptation texts and illustrated pages, and also to John Lowe, chair of the Sequential Art Department at Savannah College of Art and Design, for his assistance in pairing the right artists with the right stories.

First published in the United States of America in 2008 by Walker Publishing Company, Inc.
Distributed to the trade by Macmillan

For information about permission to reproduce selections from this book, write to Permissions, Walker & Company, 175 Fifth Avenue, New York, New York 10010

Library of Congress Cataloging-in-Publication Data
Kneece, Mark.
The twilight zone : walking distance / by Rod Serling ;
adapted by Mark Kneece ; illustrated by Dove McHargue.
p. cm.
Summary: When he gets a flat tire within walking distance of the hometown that he has not seen in twenty years, a man walks back into his own past.
ISBN-13: 978-0-8027-9714-8 • ISBN-10: 0-8027-9714-8 (hardcover)
ISBN-13: 978-0-8027-9715-5 • ISBN-10: 0-8027-9715-6 (paperback)
1. Graphic novels. [1. Graphic novels. 2. Supernatural—Fiction. 3. Time travel—Fiction.]
I. McHargue, Dove, ill. II. Serling, Rod, 1924–1975.
III. Twilight zone (Television program) IV. Title.
PZ7.7.K65Tx 2008 [Fic]—dc22 2008004273

Packaged by Design Press, a division of Savannah College of Art and Design, Inc.®
22 East Lathrop Street, Savannah, Georgia 31415

Adaptation from Rod Serling's original script by Mark Kneece
Illustrated by Dove McHargue
Color separations by Cassandra Wedeking, Andre R. Frattino, Kyle C. Ladd, Daria Makaíalohilohi, Pickard Hoey, Shawn C. Gilchrist, and Sean Toenniges
Lettering by Mia Paluzzi and Matthew Razzano
Series title treatment by Devin O'Bryan
Series copyediting by Kerri O'Hern
Series creative development by Anna Marlis Burgard and Emily Easton
Series art direction and design by Angela Rojas
Series project management by Angela Rojas and Melissa Kavonic
Creative consultant: Carol Serling

Photograph of Rod Serling © Bettmann/Corbis

Visit Walker & Company's Web site at www.walkeryoungreaders.com
Visit Savannah College of Art and Design's Web site at www.scad.edu

Printed in China
2 4 6 8 10 9 7 5 3 1 (hardcover)
2 4 6 8 10 9 7 5 3 1 (paperback)

All papers used by Walker & Company are natural, recyclable products made from wood grown in well-managed forests. The manufacturing processes conform to the environmental regulations of the country of origin.

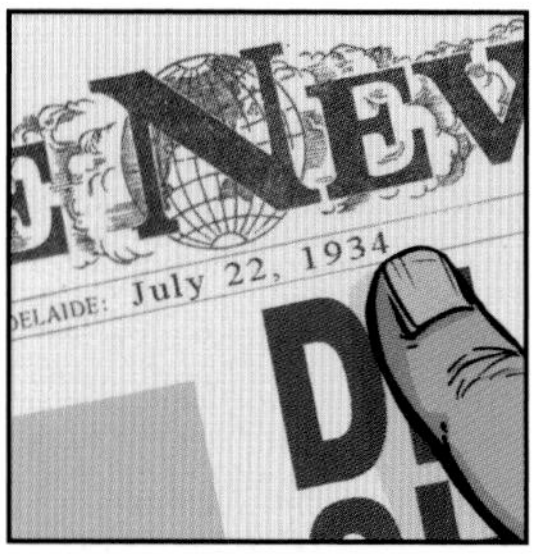
July 22, 1934